# Beginnings

## Michael E. Register

# Beginnings

By Michael E. Register

www.thebereshithchronicles.com
www.michaelregister.com

Published in Hughesville, MD, by Calamus Crest. Calamus Crest

Calamus Crest titles may be purchased in bulk for educational, business, fund-raising, or sales promotional use. For information, please e-mail SpecialMarkets@CalamusCrest.com

International Standard Book Number: 978-0-615-49242-1

Publisher's note: This novel is a work of fiction. Names, characters, places, and incidents are either products of the author's imagination or used fictitiously. All characters are fictional, and any similarity to people, living or dead, is purely coincidental.

*For Brenda,*
*Who loves me*
*In spite of it all.*

# Dramatis Personae

**Archangel** - In the hierarchy of angels, Archangel is similar to a General, or one in charge of millions.

**Azazel** - Seraphim Angel. This General, known as an excellent strategist, answers directly to Lucifer.

**Barry** - An Archeology professor at the University of Maryland, Barry works in the lab environment and knows the nitty gritty of taking samples and sending them out for testing. He runs the "lab" portions of courses and is very adept at teaching students to find truth through experimentation and rational thinking. Barry and Jessica are good friends and met when Jessica joined the department a year prior to her husband's death. Barry is married to Sara, a highly intuitive person who bases her decision-making more on spiritual meaning than physical evidence. Two more different individuals would be hard to imagine.

**Belle** - Jessica's administrative assistant, twenty-something, is a natural editor-proofreader. Belle comes from a long line of writers and hopes someday to be published.

**Cherubim** - Angels. Similar in appearance to Man. Set apart by their size, they are much larger than Man, ranging from seven to twelve feet tall. Their wingspans are large and range from twice their height to two and a half times their height.

**Elohim** - The Creator. This individual is the most mysterious of all. Being everywhere at once, and existing outside of time, this being is the one who creates life with a spoken Word. Even Elohim's names are mysteries and many are considered too sacred to write in a novel. This name, "Elohim" is considered common and therefore safe for this purpose.

**Falk** - Among the fastest of the Angels, this Cherubim is one of the smaller messenger angels. He is known to be fierce and highly unpredictable.

**Gabriel** - Archangel

**Hillel** - An Angel in Uriel's choir.

**Jeremiel** - An Angel in Remiel's Choir. Jessica sees him after he has become an Archangel.

**Jessica Mozes** - Archeologist and professor at the University of Maryland. Having lost her husband, Stephen, to a chronic illness eighteen months earlier, she finds the steady interaction with students and faculty tiring and would like nothing less than to bury herself in studies.

**Kalil** - One of the fire angels, Kalil is smaller than most of the angels in his choir and, unlike his cohorts, he displays timidity. Hillel, his closest friend, usually can pull the best from Kalil at times when most needed.

**Lucifer** - Seraphim - This red serpent/dragon was created to be the Commander of the angelic host in Paradise. He was responsible for the angels' initial training.

**Metatron** - Ancient scribe of the throne room. While he is thought of technically as an angel, he is the only being that sits in the throne room other than Elohim Himself. He was also not created at the time the other angels were created and no one knows exactly when he came to be. Some have called him, The Angel of The Lord.

**Michael** - Archangel. Bronze skin, tawny hair and fiery blue eyes, this athletically-built angel stands nine feet tall. When he appears in man-like form, he is slightly shorter, about 6' 9", olive skin and black hair. His skin tone and hair color help him to blend in with the peoples of the Middle East, where he appears most often. He is given the task of guarding the glory of the Creator's image. Therefore this angel and all the angels under his charge protect man (the Image of Elohim).

**Ophanim** - Angels. These are mysterious orb-shaped beings. They worship the Creator, in the throne room, by orbiting the throne, forming what to many people would resemble a planetary system with the throne as the fiery central sun.

**Ozel** - in Uriel's Choir, because of his immense size, this Angel would seem out of place.

**Raguel** - Archangel of Justice, this angel and his kind are dark-complected and have black raven-like wings.

**Raphael** – Archangel of Healing. Raphael's choir tends to the mental and physical wellbeing of Elohim's people. Many times they are accompanied by Ophanim Orbs.

**Remiel** - Archangel - As carrier of the sound of Paradise, this angel is charged with creating thunder when called upon.

**Sara** - Barry's wife, Sara is a spiritual and intuitive person. She can see spiritual meaning in most of the strange occurrences of life, as well as the more normal events. It's interesting that she is drawn to Barry, the more pragmatic "if I can't prove it, it's not true" type of personality.

**Satan** - Enemy of Paradise - In his quest for power and his mistrust of the Creator, Lucifer-turned-Satan became the enemy of the Kingdom of Light. Satan literally means "Enemy."

**Semyaza** - Seraphim Angel. This General answers directly to Lucifer.

**Seraphim** - Angels. These angels are the Dragon Serpents of Paradise, varying greatly in size and color. They also have varying numbers of horns and tail spikes. They started out with two wings, but over time many developed two more, then more, up to thirty wings.

**Tzadkiel** - An Angel in Remiel's Choir and later in Jeremiel's Choir.

**Uriel** - Archangel. Tasked with carrying the fire of Elohim, this Cherubim, and those he leads, are completely covered in flames and to modern man they appear to have a Far Eastern appearance, as though they had originated in China, Japan or Mongolia. They are slightly smaller than most of the other angels. In the world where Michael's angels are Eagles, Uriel's angels would be more like Hawks.

**Wilson** - The head of AMS Labwerks, Wilson has had a good working relationship with Barry through the years. He is a trusted resource.

**Zerachiel** - Archangel assigned to the protection of the children of men.

# Contents

# Prologue

*This Morning*

*"I'm not sure what to say*
*it's been so long since I've spoken with You*
*or to You*

*I don't know how to go on*
*in the day-to-day routine there is safety*
*but no warmth*

*Why am I here?*
*Why should I go on?*
*My life was taken from me on the night Stephen passed away*

*It's stupid I know*
*I can't say that he died*
*I hate that word*

*I hate it*

*we were one, half of who I was, ripped away*
*all that remains is torn, bleeding*
*confused*

*Why was I left here all alone?*
*Why did You take him and not me?*
*What is my purpose?*

*I don't know how to go on*
*Please help me*
*I beg You*

*Amen"*

## Chapter 1

# Special Delivery

The scribe held out the long cylindrical package to the messenger and whispered, "Falk, you need to get this scroll to the captain right away, he is expecting it."

"Where will I find him?"

"He is in the City of God."

Falk nodded. His dented and gashed breastplate bore the scars of prior delivery missions. He turned his back to the scribe, pulled the shield, strapped to his back, to one side allowing access to a pouch fastened underneath. The scribe opened the pouch, reached up to slide the cylinder in, then lowered the top flap and secured it.

The scribe patted Falk's shoulder, letting him know he had finished.

The messenger turned toward the edge of the temple balcony, looked over the side to judge the distance to the ground. They were several miles high and he quickly scanned the surroundings. At the base of the temple were rows of rose bushes of every conceivable color and pyre plants, who's ever moving leaves licked the air in a constant rhythmic dance.

The golden street just beyond the plants was filled with effervescent activity, as men and women walked here and there, interacting with each other, coming from or walking to various destinations, living out their eternal lives in peace. Most of the people here spent their time learning things they should have learned back on Earth, in their mortal lives. In this place, the temptations of earth could no longer distract them from their true calling, and their time was no longer wasted in vain pursuits.

He looked past the people and roadway to see the grass covered field, which was surrounded by a forest dotted with stately mansions and estates, the homes of the people, as far as he could see.

He backed away from the edge seven steps, placed his teardrop shaped headgear on his head, and turned to face the scribe. The scars on his face ended where the depressions and scratches in the helmet began. He saluted, his arm returning to his side after receiving a nod from the scribe.

Falk ran to the edge and jumped, back arched, legs together and arms extended in an elegant swan dive. His body plummeted toward the ground as he halfway unfurled two enormous wings. He kept the feathered limbs close to his body, much like a falcon would when building speed. Then with his back still arched, he angled his wings, forcing his body into an arcing path that brought him parallel with the street, the golden color reflected in his armor.

Many people on the golden road stopped what they were doing to watch the majestic being overhead. Some pointed as he flew by, others saluted.

The reflection in his armor turned green as he swooped over the grass field, his wings now fully outstretched. The tops of the tall grass followed him as he flew over. Beyond the field he raced toward a huge spiral opening in the air; the portal to another world.

He entered the portal, a swirling tunnel of light and color, many more colors than a man can see. This place, where the differing lattice work of two realities met, had a soothing effect on his nervous system. He could feel the difference in the forces acting on him as he progressed forward. The thinner or less dense reality he now infiltrated allowed for even greater speed, while the odor, that electric-metallic smell overwhelmed all other odors in this place.

He continued forward, moving past the far end of the tube and found himself in the familiar black space just above the earth, the moon moved off to his right, and for a moment, he remembered when this white heavenly body was smooth and perfect. He turned back to his target and pushed on into the stratosphere above the life-filled, blue planet.

He drifted close to fifteen minutes, his wings undulating in the solar winds, allowing time for the planet beneath him to rotate. He waited for a certain portion of the globe to appear on the horizon.

"Here it comes," He whispered to himself as he waited, and the globe continued to spin. Then, when the Indian Ocean was beneath him, he said, "The race is on."

Several final wing thrusts were all that were needed before he began the descent. Pulling his wings close to his sides, he allowed gravity to multiply his speed time and again, his entire body buffeted as the air rushed by. His helmet caught ablaze first, then his shoulders and wings, matching the fire that had been in his eyes from the beginning. Engulfed in flame, he rocketed toward the ground. To the casual observer, just another meteorite had hit the atmosphere and was being consumed by it. Perfectly comfortable in the inferno, the messenger pressed on. His expression remained stern, the package safe, strapped to the center of his back.

He streaked toward the City of God, Jerusalem. Reaching over his shoulder, he unclasped the shield and slid his right forearm through the harness, grasping the handle at the far side. Then using his left hand he pulled his sword free from its sheath, its fire blue in stark contrast to the orange flames which encased him.

Through the roar of his own flames he heard another sound building behind him, a deep menacing howl. He glanced over his left shoulder, back toward space. Nothing. He looked over his right shoulder. Two fiery streaks were following him, catching him. A third being, farther away, moved off to the east, toward ancient Persia. He moved his shield to cover his chest and most of his face while painfully contorting his body to become more aerodynamic. His speed again began to climb.

He glanced back over his shoulder, the two were faster than his best effort. He looked back to the ground he was racing toward, the roof of the Dome of the Rock only barely visible as a golden glint in the sun. He would never make it. The two behind him were within two hundred yards and still gaining.

Falk's massive wings stretched out to their full width, grabbing the air like voracious scoops. His limbs and head lunged forward, his voice cried out past clenched teeth with the strain of the almost instant slowing to a near standstill. Such deceleration was not possible for the pursuers and they barreled past him, both banking in opposite directions.

The two serpentine beasts regrouped, separated from their prey by nearly a hundred yards. The larger serpent motioned to the smaller companion to stay put, calling out, "I'll take care of this little pest."

The monster churned his gigantic leathery wings, gaining speed as he flew directly toward the messenger who had invaded their territory. Fire and smoke puffed out of flared nostrils and between bared teeth. Its head bobbed up and down with each down stroke of its wings, sending waves of motion through its torso, ending with whips of its spiked tail.

The messenger was already narrowing the gap between himself and these two interceptors. He held his shield with the top directly below his eyes. A slit remained between helmet opening and the top of the shield. He moved fast, and quickness was an ally. As the two came within fifteen yards, the dragon exhaled a brilliant stream of fire, more as a distraction than to injure. The dragon tumbled forward in the air.

The messenger, faced with the temporary cloak of flame, pulled his wings close to his body and ducked to the right. The tail spikes sailed past his body, slicing through the flames, vortexes swirling like tiny sideways tornadoes in it's wake. Falk's arm shot out to the side, the burning blade found it's target as the dragon continued its forward roll. The creature's head along with half its neck separated from the huge body, flopping end over end, spewing glowing hot liquid into the air, surreal.

The body parts sizzled and popped as they fell, releasing a thick yellow vapor, until only the vapor was left to dissipate slowly.

Falk looked toward the second dragon, who greeted him with fangs and snarling hatred. The beast was already upon him and Falk tumbled through the air, the smaller brute was now attached to him, gripping his armor and flesh with the talons of his hands and feet. The dragon's wings fought furiously to keep the invader from getting any closer to the ground. Its teeth gnawed at Falk's helmet cutting into it like a can opener. The messenger's shield bashed the creature's face up and away, knocking the jaws free as a loud multi-octave screech filled the air. His helmet, now free, toppled toward the earth.

The dragon's back erupted with blue flame, as the blade pierced through. Its screeching subsided like a siren out of air, frenetic body motions relaxed, eyes stared at nothing.

Screams and shrieks caught Falk's attention to the East. A hideous and angry mob of serpents flew toward him. He yanked the sword free from the disintegrating corpse and continued his journey to the earth. The mob was too far away to catch him now, but he knew the fighting had only just begun.

## Chapter 2

# Dr. Angelo

Jarred away from her daydreaming by a knock on her office door, Jess turned as her twenty-something administrative assistant approached her desk. Belle was a short girl of just over five feet tall with dish water blonde hair in a sort of pixie cut, pale skin, and blue eyes. She was rather thin, and while not altogether clueless, common sense was not her strong point; however, she had plenty of book smarts, which was exactly what Jess had looked for when hiring an assistant. Belle was a great team member and an excellent editor. This last point was a big help when Jess needed to submit various papers and written reports. The two had learned to work well together over the past several years.

"Good morning, Belle, what's up?" Jess asked.

Belle scanned a note in her hand, "I just got a call. Some guy would like an appointment with you this afternoon. I need to confirm that you're available today at four o'clock. Your schedule says you're free, but I just wanted to make sure."

"OK, well I think I'm free all day, except for my classes, let me double check."

As she pulled her already open appointment book out from under a pile of tests on her desk, she knocked a small framed picture over. She pushed her long dark hair over her ear while she glanced at the fallen picture, now face down. She sat the picture back up, looking at it for a moment, then quickly flipped the page to see what her agenda held for that particular day. Clearing her throat, she looked toward Belle.

"Yep, I'm free. Who is it?"

"Let's see. His name sounded Italian," Belle scanned the note again, quickly finding the name she had scribbled down. "Dr. Michael Angelo? He says he has an artifact for you to see. Do you know who he is?"

Jess quipped, "Unless he's used to painting church ceilings while lying on his back, I'd have to say I don't know who he is."

Belle's face contorted slightly as she said, "Ummm, OK, so I can set up the appointment?"

Jessica smiled, again realizing the extent to which her humor went unappreciated here in the office. "Sure, that's fine, I'll be here."

Belle rolled her eyes slightly as she turned and made her way back to her desk to finish the call.

Jessica sat her coffee down just long enough to lift her bag from the floor and onto her shoulder. It contained a textbook and several notebooks. Glancing at the clock on her desk, she picked up her mug again and headed out the door and down the hall to her first class of the day.

---

Jessica worked diligently to get the papers on her desk graded, she had sat down at one o'clock and had scarcely looked to see the time.

Belle knocked on the door as she poked her head around Jess' partially closed office door. "Jess, your four o'clock is here." Belle's eyes were wide, and she silently mouthed the words, "Oh My Gosh," then continued, "should I bring him in?"

"What? It's four already?" Jessica looked to the clock on her desk to see it was four minutes till four. "I have a couple of minutes to clean up my desk a little. Just go ahead and bring him in at four, OK?"

"OK, will do."

Jessica groaned slightly, moving the remaining two stacks of tests to the top of a cabinet to the right of her office. "I can't believe it's four already," she said, under her breath. Taking a quick peek in the mirror next to the cabinet, she let out a sigh. Snatching her purse, she quickly dug through it, finding the items needed to at least make herself presentable. She touched up her makeup and pushed her hands through her hair, sighing again, *It'll have to do.* Jess walked back to her desk just as Belle knocked once again on her door.

"Jess, this is Dr. Michael Angelo, your four o'clock appointment." Again Belle's eyes grew wide in an expression meant for her boss and no other.

"Show him in," Jessica said while moving between her leather chair and her desk.

Stepping back out the door, Belle motioned for the guest to enter the office.

He stepped in, stooping slightly to enter through the doorway. Jessica now understood Belle's expression, Dr. Angelo was massive, just fitting through the door, having bowed his head to clear the top and practically rubbing the sides on his way through, she wasn't sure, but he may have turned his body slightly to avoid the door jams. He wore a dark overcoat that covered a white dress shirt, open at the top button, and black jeans. His shoes looked like some sort of military style black leather boots with thick treaded soles. He had olive skin, with a chiseled facial structure and a scar across one cheek. He had long dark hair, which was pulled neatly into a ponytail. Belle stood behind him staring almost straight up, glancing back at her boss, her eyes wide, and again mouthed the same words as before, "OH MY GOSH."

Jessica said, "Belle, why don't you get Dr. Angelo a cup of coffee."

"No thank you, I am fine," Dr. Angelo said in a deep commanding voice that echoed in the small office.

"If you'd like, we have hot tea, soda, water?" Belle pressed.

"No thank you. Really, I *am* fine," Dr. Angelo answered.

"Thank you Belle, that will be all," Jess said.

As Belle walked out the door and back to her desk, she called out, "OK Jess, let me know if you need anything."

Motioning to one of the two thickly padded wooden chairs in front of her desk, Jessica said, "Please, have a seat Dr. Angelo. What can I do for you?"

The man moved to the front of the chair to her right side, standing next to it. After a moment he pulled an odd shaped backpack from his shoulder and moved to sit in the chair, seeming more than a little uncomfortable. Looking into her eyes he said, "Thank you for seeing me on such short notice."

She hadn't noticed his eyes before this moment, but now that she saw them she felt pierced to her core. They were a lighter royal blue and she thought she saw the color moving. She immediately began to feel a warmth flooding into her and she quickly looked away.

Dr. Angelo continued, "I represent an organization that deals in ancient artifacts of a secretive nature."

"What sort of artifacts?"

"If you do not mind, I brought one for you to have a look at." Reaching to his pack, Dr. Angelo unzipped the top and pulled out an oblong tube. It must have been 30 inches long at the very least, with finely detailed caps on either end. Dr. Angelo reached out his hand, holding out the tube for Jess to take.

Examining the tube, she became instantly aware that this was no cardboard tube used to store large diagrams or posters. This tube was made out of something much more substantial. If she were to guess, she would say it was made of leather, but she had never seen leather this hard before. Looking at the markings on the tube and caps, she quietly said, "These are Paleo Hebrew writings."

Dr. Angelo stood to his feet and said. "That is right, the Hebrew style of writing before Israel was captured by Babylon. Open it. Just pull the end open."

Carefully, Jessica pulled the cap with a slight rocking motion. The cap began to move, slowly opening with a "pop" and releasing a scent of peaches and some other spice she couldn't place. Setting the cap on the desk, Jess saw a pair of handles inside the tube, reaching in she pulled the long scroll from the tube. Dr. Angelo reached across her desk to help her, taking the tube, as she carefully pulled the last of the scroll free, along with the handles at the other end. Dr. Angelo placed the tube on the desk.

Holding the scroll carefully by the handles at either end, Jess looked toward Dr. Angelo, "What is this organization you represent?"

"That is not important right now. What *is* important is that the information in this scroll be made known to mankind. Now is the time for this to happen, and you have been chosen for this task because of your unique qualifications." Reaching down to her desk he lifted the overturned picture. "Your picture fell over, do you mind?"

Jessica squirmed a bit as the large man looked at the picture. "Yes, it fell this morning."

"I have seen this man. His name is...Stephen, right?"

"Yes, where did you see him? How did you know him?" With great care, she placed the scroll on her desk.

Dr. Angelo thought for a moment, exhaling a deep breath slowly, "He is a good man."

"Was...he was a good man," Jessica corrected him, "he passed away almost a year ago."

Dr. Angelo's countenance changed, his head and shoulders slumped. He glanced toward Jessica, "I am very sorry for your loss, Ma'am."

Sadness began to fill her eyes as Dr. Angelo handed her the picture. She looked down at it, running her fingers over the photo of her husband's face. "How did you know him?"

"I spoke with him on several occasions; he always mentioned his beautiful wife. He always spoke highly of her, of you. Again, I am so very sorry."

Jessica looked at the scroll becoming slightly dizzy. "What did you just say about the scroll?"

Dr. Angelo motioned to the scroll, "Go ahead, open it."

Jessica rolled the scroll open a few inches and touched the edge of the parchment. "I've never seen anything like this; it seems very old, I guess, yet at the same time it feels strong and tough." She opened the scroll further.

"It is upside down," the big man hinted.

"Oh, right." She quickly rolled the scroll closed, flipped it over, and unrolled it again in the right direction. Smiling she said, "I would have caught that."

Dr. Angelo smiled back, "I know."

Breaking from his gaze again, she realized she had not covered her hands. She pulled open her top left hand desk drawer then reached in to grab two white gloves from a small dispenser box in her drawer. Glancing up, her guest appeared to be unconcerned. Odd behavior for someone charged with protecting artifacts.

The scroll had opened somewhere in the middle and she began to interpret what she saw there. Moving her gloved finger from right to left across the text she read each line, then spoke out the English interpretation, "Above the seraphim was a ring of charged green swirling gas, as though emerald powder were trapped in the air as it whirled violently. From this spinning green cloud came incredible bolts of lightning, crashing all around the throne with crackling thunder exploding from the light. Around the throne were 24 smaller thrones; they were all empty and looked small enough that man could occupy them. Surrounding all this, was what appeared to be a great stadium, filled with seats, *man sized*. He wondered what the empty seats were for. Who would sit in them? Then he saw one seat filled."

Jess paused and sat down on the edge of her leather office chair, looking up at Dr. Angelo, "This looks like a description of the throne room in heaven."

Dr. Angelo stood looking into her eyes. They seemed to burn with intensity as he spoke to her. "This scroll contains part of an ancient story; one that is ready to be revealed. It is time to retell the story contained in this scroll. It's a familiar story, told in a new and expanded way. You are being given the great opportunity to distribute the words of this scroll to your society. If you choose to fulfill this mandate, more scrolls will follow."

Jessica sat for a moment, trying to understand all that was taking place in her little office. Her eyes searched the air, trying to decide if this were really true, that this man in her office was really legit, or maybe he was crazy. Maybe he made all this up. Perhaps he researched to find people who had studied Paleo Hebrew, but who would know that? How did some secret group know she could interpret this scroll? "Look, I'm going to have to think about this, I just don't know..."

"You have one week. You may handle this scroll in any way you see fit, run any tests, anything you wish. The importance is in the message on the artifact, not the artifact itself."

She looked down at the scroll itself, "How many scrolls are there?"

"Three. If you will excuse me, I will go now, and I will be back next Thursday afternoon at this same time."

"OK, I'll have an answer for you next week."

"Very well. Blessings to you," Dr. Angelo bowed slightly before turning to leave, then stooped to step through the door.

Several seconds had passed before Belle came slinking into the office, "Geez, that guy was huge! Tall dark and handsome, just the way you like 'em!"

Jess crossed her arms and stared at Belle in mock contempt. "Isabella! Don't start with me."

Belle approached Jess' desk, looking at the opened scroll, "Oh wow, is that what he wanted you to look at?"

"Yeah, that's it. It's pretty interesting. I'll have to do some digging to see where it fits in the dating records. It's very complex with all these engravings. See how intricate the work is? It looks very old." Jess pivoted in her chair, then stood to look out the window. Several students walked along the winding concrete pathway toward the parking area, apparently finished for the day. "Belle, can you get Barry Isaacs on the phone for me?"

"Ummm, sure no problem." Belle disappeared from the office and in a few moments called from her desk, "Barry is on line two!"

"Thanks Belle!" Jess turned to pick up the phone, selecting the second button. "Barry?"

Barry finished packing his brief case as he spoke. "Yes, Hi Jess. I was just about to head out, what's up?"

"I'm sorry to keep you. Just a quick question."

"Sure, ask away!"

"OK, I have a scroll that I want to date."

"You want to date a scroll? You know there are plenty of men that would love to date you."

"Ha Ha Ha. Very funny. My heart is taken, you know that."

"Yes, I know. So you have a scroll you want to date. I'm assuming since you're calling me about this you'll want the carbon-14 testing done. I can take the samples here and send them out to the testing lab; however, I need to tell you, carbon-14 dating can only be performed on organic material. So, this scroll you have, are any of the components organic-say, wooden handles or parchment made from animal hide of some kind?

"You know, I'm looking at it, and I can't tell. May I bring it down to you tomorrow to have a look? Will you be in?"

"Sure, I'll be in tomorrow. I only have a ten o'clock class. Other than that, I'll be catching up on some work in the lab, so I'll be around. Oh, and I'm meeting my wife for lunch."

"OK, how does two o'clock sound?"

"Perfect. Then I'll see you around two. See ya tomorrow."

"Bye Barry, thanks!" She hung up the phone and sat down at her desk, leaned way back and stared at the ceiling. *What is all this about? Dr. Angelo, who is he? I guess I'll find out soon enough if the scroll is real. At least I'll know that much before deciding.*

"Good night Jess," Belle said as she walked past Jessica's office door.

"G'night Belle. See ya tomorrow."

## Chapter 3

# A Closer Look

"Where'd you get this?" Barry held out the tube with both hands, letting it bob up and down, measuring its weight. "Wow, pretty hefty."

Jessica was hesitant to explain. "I'm not sure you're going to believe this, but a man named 'Dr. Angelo' came to my office and gave it to me. He wants me to interpret it. Says it's a story the world needs to hear."

Barry replied with a light chuckle, "Oh really? Did you put a white coat on him and have someone escort him out with a net?"

"No, and it would have taken more like four or five guys. Anyway, he said he represents a group that protects ancient secrets or artifacts like this one. Something like that."

Barry studied the details of the engravings, tracing his finger over them. "Hmmm, I'll say this much. These engravings are very interesting, the detail is amazing. So, why did he give it to *you*? Don't these things usually go through the Dean? I mean, no offense, but you're one of the newer teachers in the department."

Jessica sat on one of the lab's stools, across from Barry, leaning with her elbows on the table. "No, I know, I mean, I don't know." She shrugged. "He said his group chose me because I have 'unique qualifications.' I can read the inscriptions. Maybe that's what he meant. I have a week to decide if I'll take the job."

Barry continued his close examination of the outer tube and caps. He glanced up over his glasses, "Make the world read this scroll?"

"I suppose I would interpret it and publish it. Summer vacation is right around the corner. I'm not teaching summer classes, so I could do it then. I'm planning to spend the summer at a house my parents own in Colorado. I could do it there. First, I want to know the age of the scroll, to lend some credence to this."

"So you've obviously thought about this in a serious manner." Barry took a deep breath and eased the air back out in a slow sigh. He set the tube down on a sample tray.

"So, what's your cut?"

"My cut?"

"Yeah, as in pay. He did say his group would pay you, right?"

"He didn't mention it, and I didn't think to ask; it was all rather sudden. I can ask him next week. The real question is whether it's something I want to do."

Barry removed his glasses and turned to face Jess. "True, but be sure you ask. You wouldn't want to go through this whole exercise and get next to nothing for it. Jess, look at me."

She turned her eyes back toward him, sensing a lecture coming on.

He continued, "I know you love this sort of thing, and diving back into study for the summer sounds appealing, especially for someone who doesn't want to face the world right now, but... you need to know the fine print on something like this."

"Yeah, you're right. He also mentioned more scrolls, and if I get this one done, he'll bring the next one." She rested her head on her hands. "Don't know what to think." She paused for several seconds before quietly saying, "There was something about his eyes."

"Did you say his eyes?"

"Yeah, his eyes. I've never seen anything like his eyes before."

"What do you mean?"

"I don't know. Something different about them, as if they were warm...geez! This doesn't make any sense!"

Barry crossed his arms, "Look, let's get this thing tested. Either way, at least some of your questions will be answered."

"You're right. Tell me what you need again."

"For carbon-14 testing, I'll need to remove a sample of whichever parts I test."

Jess sat up once again. "No problem, he said I could do whatever I saw fit to do to the scroll."

Barry glanced back toward the parchment. "Ok, I'll get to work. I have to admit, I'm intrigued. I'll try to get the samples today, and hopefully, the lab can run tests on Monday. Cross your fingers. When they finish, I'll let you know right away. You should have plenty of time to make an informed decision."

"Good, that's good," her head nodded slowly. "I really appreciate this, Barry." She glanced at him, now with a sideways grin.

He laughed, "Yeah, the whole world will owe me once you get this interpreted!"

She slid from the stool, "Very funny. I gotta get back to my grading. Tell Sara hello for me."

"Will do. Take it easy this weekend. Try not to think about all this. We'll get it sorted out."

She gave Barry a friendly hug before walking toward the door. "See you next week."

# Chapter 4

# The Sample

Barry worked the stretchy latex onto his hands, pulling the gloves firmly between his fingers. He carefully opened the case, placing the cap on the freshly-cleaned stainless steel table, and held down the case with one hand, slowly pulled the scroll out and placed it next to the cap. Many minutes passed as he studied the items, first using only his glasses. *Hmmm, where did you come from?* He walked across the lab to another table, picked up a large lighted magnifying glass affixed to a table stand, and brought it to the sample. Plugging it in and flipping on the light, he continued to study the finely detailed scroll handles. Pressing the red button on a small digital voice recorder, he began to dictate.

"Artifact number 2177 consists of an oblong tube with the appearance of stiff leather. The case is covered with highly ornate engravings. There are two stone end caps. The caps are intricately engraved, much like the tube. The tube and caps are a casing for a scroll with stone handles of unknown type and origin, very heavy. The parchment of the scroll is a weighty, thick material and, while appearing very old, does not appear to exhibit the brittleness normally associated with items from antiquity. All parts of this artifact appear to be quite robust.

"The casement tube is engraved with four scenes. The first depicts a large central figure, like a sun or star. Clouds or smoke surround this central light. It appears to be a representation of space or the universe or something. Lots of smaller bodies surround the central figure, and they form, let's see, *one, two, three, four, five, six, seven,* seven curved tails, sort of like a spiral galaxy.

"The second scene, shows what looks like curved wisps of some sort, quite a few of them, on top of what appears to be a great body of water. The foreground depicts a singular figure, a man, standing before a remarkably rendered, winged, dragon-looking thing, I suppose. In the background, the same central figure as in the first scene, a central sun, surrounded by radiating clouds.

"Moving on to the third scene, like the first two, this one has the same central figure, showing the sun and radiating smoke. These elements are surrounded by some sort of beings, also radiating out around the central figure, completely filling the scene. The focus is a figure lying face down on the ground. The details are elaborate. The figure looks as if it might be part of the ground.

"The final scene does not show the central figure. This would be a fairly typical battle scene if not for the level of detail. The battle is between many of the dragon creatures, like the one in the first scene, and, well, men with wings, angels I suppose. On either end of the scene the dragons are being thrown down a cliff of some sort. There seems to be a mixture, a few of the angels are being thrown down, and a few of the dragons seem to be throwing others down."

Barry replaced the casement tube on the table, then turned to the scroll and resumed speaking into the recorder. "In an attempt to learn the approximate age of sample 2177, I will now remove a portion of the parchment. I'm using the word *parchment* only because I don't know what else to call it. This material is unlike anything I've seen before. This sample is much thicker than the normal calf skin or goat skin used in making parchment."

Barry reached over to his instrument tray and grabbed a pair of new surgical scissors, long-handled, with short blades at the end. He leaned toward the recorder. "I will now cut the parchment material at the bottom end of the scroll on the right hand side." He placed the scissors at the end of the parchment and eased the blades down onto the material.

"The material is very difficult to cut, and a clear fluid is coating the scissors as I go... However, I am able to make slow progress. I'm cutting approximately one square centimeter to be used for dating purposes. This should be much more than AMS Labwerks will need to perform their testing."

He continued his belabored cutting as he continued, "I chose this portion of the artifact because it contains the writing and should therefore give the closest date to when the writing took place. We have no idea if these are the original handles or when the case was made, so this seems like the best bet." Barry finished the last snip, "I've just completed taking the sample." Upon removing the scissors Barry noticed indentions in his now tender fingers, as though he had been cutting for quite some time.

"It must have been tougher than I thought."

He placed the scissors aside. "Ok, I've removed the sample portion and more of the clear fluid is on the table directly beneath the cuts I made. The fluid doesn't appear to be caustic, I'm rubbing the end of the scissors in the fluid, and it has an oily consistency. I'm going to collect the fluid for further testing."

Barry plucked a piece of gauze from his work tray and leaned to the microphone. "I'm now soaking up the fluid with a piece of gauze. I'm placing the gauze into a vial for testing."

Barry stuffed the gauze into a tall vial and the parchment sample into another vial, sealing both with rubber caps. He walked across the lab to grab a couple of labels, pulled the pen from his lab coat, and quickly scribbled the contents of each vial onto a label. He moved back across the lab as he peeled the labels, sticking one to each of the vials. "Ok, both samples are identified and ready to be sent off. I'm placing a cloth over the cut portion of the scroll to soak up any extra fluid that may be there." He took a large gauze piece from the instrument tray and glanced at the scroll to place the gauze over the cut.

Barry's eyes grew wide as he viewed the parchment, "What the...?"

## Chapter 5

# The Phone Call

Jessica arrived short of breath. She had practically run down the steps and to Barry's office, a few doors from the lab. She knocked. No answer.

"Hi Jess!" Barry's voice came from behind her. He was hurrying. "Thanks for coming, there's something in the lab I want you to see, but we need to hurry." Also out of breath, he fumbled with his keys, then finally pushed the right one into the knob. He quickly unlocked the door and made his way in, Jess in tow. He propped the door open and walked over to one of the stainless steel cabinets pulling out a wide drawer containing a tray with the scroll, tube, and caps.

"Can you help me-Here, grab this? Let's place it on that table there." Jess and Barry lifted the tray and carefully placed it on top of the adjacent table. He pulled a stool over for her while with the other hand he closed the cabinet behind them.

"OK, Whew!"

"Hi Barry, you said I needed to see something?"

"Right, OK, I came in on Saturday to prepare the sample for the lab to test, and I was able to send off the samples this morning."

"Great!"

"Yeah, but that's not why you're here. Something very interesting happened when I took the sample-two things happened actually. First, when I cut the sample, the parchment oozed a fluid."

"What sort of fluid?"

"I'm not sure yet, I collected a sample and sent it to the lab this morning as well. So we're waiting on two tests."

"Fluid came out of the parchment?"

"Yeah, I know, it's unbelievable, but then something else happened!"

"What?"

"Once I had the samples all ready to go, I came back to the scroll. I had a piece of gauze to try to dry it before rolling it back up."

"But it's not rolled up." Jess pointed to the scroll.

"That's right, I left it exactly as it was. Notice anything strange about it?"

Jess looked at the scroll carefully. Nothing seemed odd.

"Jess, where did I cut the scroll?"

"I don't know, you'll have to unroll it more to show me." She thought for a moment as she studied it. "Wait, you just said you left it as it was, so you cut somewhere here on the scroll?"

"Yep, that's right. I cut at the bottom portion of the scroll on the right-hand side. See, it looks like it was never cut. AMS LabWerks should call any time now. I put a rush on the samples."

"No way, the piece you cut from grew back. Did you tell them that?"

"Do I look stupid? Of course not! I told them I needed the results as quickly as possible. It worked out because they said so far they've got a light week."

"So, we wait for the results."

"Let's go to my office to wait. Sara's coming by and should be here any moment. She's interested in this too."

"Who's ever heard of artifacts growing back?"

"Yeah, she has a wild theory. I'll let her tell you about it."

"Ok, it'll be good to see her again, anyway."

---

The phone rang as Barry and Jess entered his office. He motioned for Jess to have a seat while he picked up the receiver. "MSU Archeology Department... Barry Isaacs speaking... Sure I can hold."

"Where's your assistant?" Jess asked.

"Oh, I sent her home for the day..." Barry shuffled through a file folder on his desk.

"Did I miss any news?" Sara said, poking her head into the door.

He looked up. "No, I'm on the phone with LabWerks now. Have a seat, honey."

Jess patted the arm of the next chair for Sara to sit by her. "Hi Sara, he's just on hold."

"Hi." Sara sat down beside Jess.

"Yes... Yes... Sure I'm sitting down," Barry pulled his chair up behind his knees and sat on the front edge. "Wait, before you begin, may I put you on speaker?" He paused before pressing the speaker button. "Ok, Wilson I have Jessica Mozes here with me. She's a teacher here in the archeology department, and the artifact in question came from someone she is in contact with. And my wife Sara is here as well."

"Hello Sara, and Jessica, nice to meet you two."

"Hello Wilson," Sara replied.

"Hi Wilson, and please just call me Jess."

"I'll get the first item out of the way." Over the speaker the three could hear a bit of shuffling before Wilson continued, "Ok, let's talk quickly about the fluid sample. It contains Palmitic acid, Stearic acid, arachidic acid, behenic acid, myristic acid, and lignoceric acid. All are saturated fats. It also contains unsaturated and polyunsaturated fats. I don't want to go down the whole list but I can tell you right off, it's an oil. To be specific, olive oil, very *very* pure olive oil."

Barry interrupted. "It's just olive oil?"

"Yeah, that's all. How olive oil came flowing out of the parchment is a mystery, but it *is* olive oil. Something to note, the other sample you sent over is covered in the oil, so I'm not sure if it was because of sloppy handling or what."

Barry raised his eyebrows, thinking, *Maybe I should have told him*, "Wilson, the oil came from the second sample. Have you ever heard of that?"

The speaker phone was silent for several seconds. "No, never. Of course we've never had a sample like this either."

"How about you tell us what you found with the parchment sample? How old is it?"

"Ok, let me start by saying that this sample has our entire lab baffled. After cleaning the sample thoroughly, we had to split it apart to take a smaller sample from the center, to be sure there were no contaminates. To make a long story short, we had to burn the sample. During the burn cycle we compared the ratio of carbon-14 atoms given off to the carbon-12 atoms given off. This ratio is used to date the piece. Do you all understand so far?"

Sara spoke up, "Wilson, this is Sara. I must be the only one who doesn't understand this process but I don't understand how the ratio of these atoms tells an age."

Wilson replied, "No problem, Sara. here's how it works: carbon-14 is a rare form of carbon, which is continually formed in the upper atmosphere, then as it sinks to the lower atmosphere it decays into nitrogen-14. This continual cycle means there is a pretty constant level of carbon-14 available. You might ask, what does this have to do with dating old objects? Let me tell you. Living things take in or ingest things, be it the air, food, water, or minerals. All of the ingestible things contain about the same level of carbon-14 as the atmosphere. Therefore, the living thing, the thing that is eating, drinking, and breathing, also contains approximately the same level of carbon-14 as the atmosphere. When this living thing dies, it stops eating, drinking, and breathing, and therefore stops absorbing carbon-14. The carbon-14 in the body begins to diminish at a known rate, changing into nitrogen-14. We have tables and charts for the rate at which the carbon-14 level decreases. Because of this 'known' rate, we can determine how long something has been dead, as long as it has been dead at least one hundred years and no longer than fifty thousand years. We compare carbon-14 to carbon-12 because carbon-12 does not diminish, and therefore, the level of carbon-12 remains constant. Does this make sense?"

"I think so..." Sara nodded. "So you're comparing the levels of a decreasing atom to the levels of a constant, right? Carbon-14 being the decreasing atom and carbon-12 being the constant."

"That's correct."

"Ok, then why," Sara continued, "are you limited to between one hundred years and fifty thousand years?"

The voice on the speaker phone again explained, "If the sample died less than one hundred years ago, the carbon-14 in the sample hasn't had enough time to decrease enough for us to measure it very well. With any sample over 50,000 years, the carbon-14 is already depleted to a point we have a hard time making good measurements. On either end of the time scale we encounter measurement problems."

"I think I understand." Sara answered.

"Good, now remember I said that if anything is over fifty thousand years old, we cannot determine the age; however we can still measure carbon-14. It's diminished but not exhausted. Now for the kicker. In the sample you gave us, there was no Carbon-14."

"So... you couldn't measure any?"

"We didn't measure a single atom, Barry. Not only that, but we measure the carbon atoms while burning the sample. Your sample didn't burn, which could explain why we saw no carbon-14."

"What do you mean, it didn't burn?"

"Let me rephrase that: it burned, it actually burned very hot, but the fire produced no carbon-14 or carbon-12." There was a pause with static from the speaker phone.

"You're not telling us something, what is it?" Barry asked.

Wilson continued, "We've never had a sample that burned without being scorched. I mean, we burn samples until there's nothing left to burn. The sample you gave us showed no evidence it had been burned at all! As it stands now, it's back in the vial you brought it in, and other than being split apart, it shows no signs of damage at all."

Barry crossed his arms and sat on the edge of the desk, looking more than a little puzzled, "So what does that mean for dating the sample?"

Wilson sounded apologetic. "The only answer I have for you is that it is an organic sample, and the testing was inconclusive. I can't give you an age. The sample has to be consumed during the burn and your sample burned for two hours with no change whatsoever. Therefore, we cannot come up with an age."

Jessica leaned forward uneasily in her chair, "I'm not sure this helps me, I just wanted to know if the scroll was old. Knowing the age could potentially fall outside of the range possible for carbon-14 testing. You're saying you have no idea how old it is?"

Wilson answered flatly, "That's right. I wish I had a different answer for you. Officially, sample 2177 has no age or is dateless."

With a frustrated look, Barry placed his finger on the telephone's speaker button, "Wilson, we appreciate your efforts, we'll get back with you later."

"Sorry we couldn't help more."

"No problem my friend, bye."

Barry pushed the button, ending the call. He sat upright, studying the ceiling and shaking his head slightly, his arms again crossed on his chest.

"May I say something?" Sara asked sheepishly. Receiving no response she continued, "I have a theory, and this may be as good a time as any to throw it out on the table."

Jessica looked toward Sara, "Barry mentioned that. Go ahead."

"Well... he's not all that comfortable with my idea, but it looks like your investigation isn't telling you much."

Barry nodded his head. "True on both accounts."

"Ok," Sara paused a moment and inhaled deeply. "What if this man who brought you the scroll isn't a man at all?"

Jessica shook her head, "What do you mean, like he's a woman? I saw him, he was very much a man."

"No, not a woman. I know you saw him, and I'm sure he looked like a man. But can you explain anything about this scroll?"

"No. But what does that have to do with his being a man or not?"

"You've tried to date it, and your attempt was frustrated. In the Bible are plenty of places where people are approached by angels; some of the angels even taught man in the early days. Tradition holds that Michael the Archangel taught Moses, which is how Moses wrote the book of Genesis."

"Right, I know Genesis, so what are you saying? That Dr. Angelo is an Angel?"

"No, I'm not saying he is, I'm only saying...it's a possibility. I mean, who's to say angels don't still teach man? Maybe this is an angelic attempt to teach us again or to help us into the next phase of mankind or something."

"I don't know if I like the sound of that," Jessica replied.

"We all beat around the bush about this with you, Jess, but I'm going to come out with it. You know Moses suffered huge losses before the angel taught him. He had been raised as an Egyptian and so had lost his Hebrew culture. Then as a prince he discovered his Hebrew roots and, therefore, lost his royal identity. He was banished from Egypt after killing a guard and lost the only home he had known. Then he was stuck in the wilderness for forty years before returning to Egypt to lead his people to the Promised Land. He had to confront the world's greatest empire as a shepherd. He experienced great loss before his mission began. And we know you have experienced great loss as well."

Jessica grew impatient, "Stop it. Just because Stephen died doesn't mean God is sending angels to instruct me to perform some great work or save the world."

"It doesn't mean that, but He does choose those with great loss, those that have lost some degree of hope, to redirect them into something great. The loss of Stephen could have been the signal of a time of transition for you. Things could obviously be different, and they have been, but now maybe it's a time for you to bloom into more than you ever thought possible. If this visitor is some sort of an angel, and this is an assignment from heaven, God has not asked you to change the world, He only asked you to interpret a scroll, and distribute the interpretation- heck, you can even self publish it as a book. That could be all He's asking you to do, right? *If* this visitor is- some sort of an angel."

Barry looked through a thick book he had picked up from his desk, finally, with a groan, reaching the item he was searching for.

"What's that?" Jessica asked.

"My dictionary. Something Wilson said has been bothering me, a word he used. He described the scroll as 'dateless.' So I thought I would look up the precise meaning."

"So why the groan?"

"Because what Sara is talking about seems to fit. This says, 'Dateless: Having no date whatsoever; so ancient that no date can be determined; having no limits in time; timeless.' It fits what Wilson said about the sample, and it sounds like the definition of eternal."

Jessica picked up her purse and rose to leave.

"I'm getting butterflies in my stomach. This is getting weird. I'm gonna go. I have to think this over. I'll talk with you two later, but thanks for sharing your thoughts."

Sara stood. "Thanks for listening."

"I'm sorry. I'm just a little overwhelmed, and it is getting late."

Sara gave Jessica a hug and walked her to the door. "If you need anything just call, ok?"

"Will do. I just need some time alone. I'll see you two later."

"Bye Jess," Barry said, still seated at his desk.

———————

Walking back to her office a familiar numbness filled her head. She had felt this before, right after Stephen had passed. A sensation unlike any she had felt before that time-she couldn't feel anything. She tried to imagine what would cause this. Maybe a neurological shock response of some sort, maybe when the mind has too much to deal with the system stops taking in input.

She entered her office, switched on the light, and rounded her desk. Reaching out, she lifted the picture of Stephen and, holding it with both hands, began to cry. She whispered, "I miss you so much."

She turned to the window, but the reflection of the office in the glass kept her from seeing the night sky. She placed the picture into her purse, slid the strap onto her shoulder, and walked out. She didn't know where she was going, only that she needed to get away.

About two and a half hours later she found herself sitting in her car, in the parking lot of the Cove Point lighthouse. She usually came here to think or, for the last year, to cry. She grabbed a blanket from the rear hatch of her car and walked to the beach. She followed the sand, walking north for about fifty yards. The beach was accessible along the tree line, and she found her usual place amongst the pine trees looking out over the Chesapeake Bay. As it swept by every half minute or so, the glow from the lighthouse was comforting in the dark. It had always seemed like an immovable sentinel, a protector in the night.

She sat in the midst of a battle, with the humidity working hard to retain the warmth from the day and the bay breeze trying to push the heat away. She enjoyed the feeling of both, as each force seemed to win for a few moments, only to be overtaken by the other. The back and forth cycle was refreshing on her face and she loved the feeling of her hair being lifted by the wind.

The moon, a waxing crescent shape, looked as though it were going somewhere, heading off in some direction, trying to reach some goal. Glancing above the moon, staring into the depths of space, she spoke to the One everyone speaks to at some point in their lives.

"I don't know what to think about all this," she said under her breath. "You know I never blamed You for Stephen's death. I *have* stopped talking to You over the past year. I'm sorry for that. Sorry now. Maybe I was angry with You. Maybe I still am." Removing the picture from her purse, she held it in front of her. She couldn't see very well in the darkness but didn't need to see it. The image was etched into her heart. Tears rolled down her face in an unrestrained stream. "I don't want to be angry anymore. I don't know if that scroll is from You, and I don't know if I'll ever *really* know. I have heard many times that You like a good mystery, and You like for us to decide with our whole being, not just our minds." She sat for the better part of an hour, searching the night sky and listening to the waves on the shore.

"I think I'm deciding to interpret the scroll." She continued to sit for a few more minutes gazing at the moon, then looked higher into the sky once more and said, "Ok, I'll do it."

## Chapter 6

# The Trip Back

The night erupted with brightness as if by a prolonged lightning strike. The trees, the pale sand in front of her, even the ocean seemed to be lit to a brightness beyond that of daylight. Startled, she looked quickly to her right, in the direction of the lighthouse, and saw a large white light undulating with life, seemingly radiating a very bright multi-spectrum fire.

She collapsed to the ground, the strength in her legs gave way, and she found herself flat on the blanket, unhurt. She willed herself back up to her knees and sat to one side, on her right hip. As her eyes adjusted she could see that the blaze was moving toward her, the brightness decreasing until she could see that it was a very large person walking toward her, though descending through the air. The being's features were coming into view as it continued to approach. Being at least 20 feet tall and wearing a golden colored armor breast plate, the massive winged man continued toward her, unhurried. He held a shield in his left hand and a blazing sword in his right. His head was covered in a tawny-colored hair. The light began to recede, vacuuming down into a smaller, more man-size structure, though still larger than any man she had ever met.

Shaky, she wiped the tears from her face as the being drew closer, the brightness now replaced by a dark overcoat, and the tawny hair had become raven as well, until she could see the same blue eyes she had seen in her office.

"You!"

"Yes, Sara was right."

"Why didn't you just tell me?"

"You had to decide with your heart, from the core of your being, not because of external motivation." Gesturing toward the blanket Dr. Angelo said, "Please, stay seated. I am *now* able to talk with you about a few things."

Jessica settled herself, and Dr. Angelo sat next to her. "I can't believe I'm sitting here with an angel."

"We are all around you. There are many more of us than you think. A few of us have been watching you and helping you from before the time of Stephen's illness."

She sat quietly thinking. "You said earlier, in my office, that Stephen *is* a good man. You meant to say it like that, didn't you."

"Yes, I have only talked with him in the past year though we watched him all through his illness, comforting him. He's watching you and others he still cares about from his former life. He is among a vast cloud of mankind watching their descendants, cheering your people on, as well as petitioning on your behalf."

"Petitioning, what do you mean?"

"His petitions are at least partially the reason you have the scroll in your possession. He was very vocal that you would be the right choice."

Again tears rolled down her cheeks, as he spoke of Stephen, still rooting for her. She looked down at the picture she still held tight to her chest. She pulled it away just enough to look at it again. "It would be just like him to push for my advancement, believing in me." She sniffed and brushed the tears from her eyes.

"He looks much better than that now, you know."

"What do you mean?"

"He is full of life now. That picture you are holding shows him in the first stages of the illness. He looks much better now, *perfect* really."

She smiled through her tears, one finger tracing the edge of the dime store metal frame that held her husband's picture. He had been a tall man, six foot two if he stretched a little. She loved his short brown hair and eyes and his neatly cropped full beard. He was a man who loved her more than she felt deserving of. She looked to the night sky, remembering how he looked at her, or more, how he looked into her. It was as though he could see what no one else could see. He saw her, not the walls she had erected to protect herself from the world. He saw the jewel inside the lump of coal. Knowing how valuable that jewel made the coal. She closed her eyes, remembering how he spoke with her.

---

"What do you see?" she asked.

Stephen thought for a moment. "I see the one I love."

"You're just being romantic again."

"No, I'm not. I see you on the inside."

They sat looking into each others eyes. Time sped by, no one noticed.

His eyes began to soften, the inside corners of his eyebrows raised, tears began to flow down his cheeks. He spoke quietly, "You know what really sucks about dying?"

Her tears followed his. She continued looking into his eyes, barely able to shake her head back and forth.

"What really sucks about dying is that I know what it'll do to you." He looked away, "Please Jess, don't be angry when it happens... I know God has something...something big...for you. I know there's something great that only you can do." Taking her hands, he looked back into her eyes, "I wish I could be here to see it, to experience it with you." He looked down at his hands holding hers. "I know I can't, I won't be here for that, somehow my death will change you."

"How do you know that?"

"I don't know how I know. I just know."

---

She looked at Michael, her eyes had become a pair of flowing rivers, "He knew I would be angry. He asked me not to be angry."

"I remember that conversation. I was there in the room with you both. The things he said to you were things I had revealed to him. I placed those things in his mind as he slept."

"Why would you cause him such grief? Why not just let him die in peace."

"He had many questions. Sometimes it is better to let a person know what is coming, let them see the hope that is ahead, rather than let them wonder. I suppose that answer doesn't comfort you right now."

They sat in silence for several hours, watching the stars and listening to the water lap on the shore.

---

The sky had changed from black to dark blue, then to light blue, then the tiny yellow burning light began making its way above the horizon, growing as it progressed.

Jessica sat with her blanket pulled up around her. Michael sat with his knees pulled up in front of him, his powerful arms wresting on top of them. He was unaffected by the cold, though wisps of his hair were held air born in the morning breeze.

"So, now that I know you're an angel, should I still call you Dr. Angelo?"

"You can call me Michael."

"As in...the *archangel* Michael?"

"No other angel is named Michael."

As the sun continued to rise, Jessica watched Michael. She noticed he stared at the sun without blinking. "It's glorious isn't it?" She asked the large angel.

He hesitated slightly before muttering a short, "Yes."

"Why did you hesitate?"

Michael spoke without diverting his gaze from the fiery ball. "Your kind has no idea what you've lost. This entire world suffers from the fall you inflicted on it. Even this sunrise, as glorious as it is, is but a dim shadow of its former glory. Sin has changed everything...made everything pale, gray and lifeless. I have to appear this way with your kind because you can not even look into my light, and yours was brighter by far in the beginning. Your kind outshone the angels and had no need for the sun."

She didn't know what to say, continuing to look at him she could see the same sadness she had seen in her office.

Michael rose to his feet, holding his hand out to help her up, "It is time for you to head back. You have just enough time to get back to the office before class."

Jess looked at her watch, quickly rising to her feet, "I completely forgot about my class today. I don't have time to get back. Class starts in thirty minutes, and I'm at least two hours away!"

"Relax Jessica, you won't be driving."

———————

Jessica blinked her eyes and found herself in her office. Michael was standing looking out the window. She looked at the clock on her desk, which showed she had twenty-eight minutes before class would start. "I haven't showered, and my hair is a mess!"

Michael spoke calmly, "You will be OK. Your brush is in your purse."

Jessica quickly grabbed the brush from the bottom of her purse and headed to the mirror. "OK, Michael, it looks like I'll be able to get started with the scroll in a few weeks, once classes are out for the summer."

"Very well. You will see me again before you begin." Michael turned from the window, "Blessings to you, Jessica. Know that we are watching and helping." With a slight bow, he faded from view.

A surprised Belle poked her head in the door, looking to see who was talking. "Jess?"

"Good morning, Belle." Jess said as she brushed her hair.

A puzzled look covered Belle's face, "Good morning. I thought I heard voices. When did you get here? I've been here for a while now, and I didn't see you come in."

"I just...got in."

A bewildered expression covered Belle's face, "How? I was right outside your door."

Jessica shook her head, "You wouldn't believe me if I told you. I need to get some makeup on and be in class in 20 minutes."

## Chapter 7

# *Different Surroundings*

Barry had convinced her that it was a good idea. Moving, just for the summer, mostly to free her of the distractions of her life in Maryland. After all, she had only three months to work through the scroll and couldn't afford much in the way of the normal day-to-day interactions if she were to make that deadline. Interpretation is a very involved process, and this project had more to it, having to form the interpretation into a novel. Belle had pretty much invited herself. Jessica had welcomed the idea of having a familiar face along to help with the editing and formatting. Belle had proven to be very good in the past and could also provide good company.

The two had flown into the Denver airport, taken the underground shuttle from the gate to the terminal, and caught a van service that would take them right into Colorado Springs. Once in "The Springs," as the local folks called it, they took a taxi up into the mountains west of the city. The trip up the mountains was beautiful, if a little cool and dry, compared to Maryland. They saw several deer as the taxi took them up highway 24, through the pass. The 50 minute trip from "The Springs" went by too quickly, as they drove through Woodland Park, the last major town on their trip. The driver was sure to point out the local Walmart, as well as the Safeway and the smaller City Market. She pointed out the local movie theater and several restaurants. Having a female driver was nice, as men tended to be all about getting to the destination quickly without saying a word. Having some reference points would be helpful in the coming weeks.

Passing Woodland Park the driver insisted on taking them to Divide's, the smaller town's center, where there was another grocery store, "good for those times when just a few things are needed." The driver pointed out the county road they would be on as they drove by, and in just a few minutes, they were pulling into the Divide Venture Foods. The small strip mall looked similar to something out of the old west. The trees had subsided some time back, and the rolling hills dotted with cattle, deer, and elk were an amazing site. She'd never seen elk before, let alone thought she would see them grazing alongside domestic cattle. Pike's peak was to the southwest, just about 5,000 feet above their current elevation of 9,200, the top covered in snow. The driver pulled through the parking lot and out to the left onto County Road 5, making a left at the light heading back the way they came. Time to get them to their destination.

Pulling onto County Road 25, past the very small lot selling used cars, tractors, and go carts, an odd combination, Jess thought to herself. The cab traveled about a mile and a half along the dusty dirt road, winding from the rolling hills back into the trees. Various homes were along the way, maybe six or seven. The car slowed as it reached a paved driveway, the slightly cracked and grayed black top showed it's age and the effects of the harsh winters. The home was difficult to see from the road and looked small up close.

The car parked, and the three began unloading the cab, carrying the luggage up to the very small front porch. Jessica paid the taxi driver, waving goodbye, and thinking about how helpful she had been, both getting them this far and as a makeshift guide. Looking through her purse she found the keys to the home, walked back up to the porch, and slid the key into the deadbolt, unlocking it and the door knob in turn. The two moved into the house, leaving the luggage outside, finding colors straight out of the seventies-pastels, lots of them. The entryway was a sea-foam color, and as they continued into the home, the pair was met with baby blues, rose, and pastel orange.

"Wow, how long did you say it had been since your parents were here?"

"I'm not sure, but I'm pretty sure they were here last summer."

"You've never been here?"

"Nope. I think we need to do something about this color. I'm going to call them later. If they don't mind, I say we change it."

The descending stairs cut the living room in two. The larger portion had a seating area, fireplace, and a larger than normal window that overlooked the woods and distant mountain peaks. The smaller section had been utilized as a pair of built in desks. One large countertop covering short cabinets, giving each of the two desk positions ample space to spread out and work. Above was plenty of space with both open book shelves and closed cabinets.

Belle moved through the space, trailing her right hand fingers along the "desk's" countertop and stopped at the end where the second large window looked out with a similar view as the window in the living room.

"This desk area is great. It should work out real well."

"Yeah, that's pretty cool, and the views here are amazing!"

---

The two settled in. Jessica moved into the master bedroom on the upper floor, and Belle moved into an ample bedroom in the finished basement. Each had their own living space complete with full bathrooms, so they could have a sense of privacy while sharing the home. A small study was across the hall from Jessica's room where another desk was set up. She would use this room when she needed to be alone, usually when she would translate particularly tough passages.

They spent the evening getting their shared desk in order. Each had Mac laptops, and Belle would be heading into town in the morning for paper and other supplies.

Jessica finished setting up her side of the desk and wandered into the kitchen. "It's dinner time, and we have no food. Let's go out."

"OK, let me just finish up here. I'll just be a couple of minutes."

"I'll get the truck started." Jessica opened the kitchen drawer closest to the garage door. Two sets of car keys were there, one for each of her parents. She took a set from the drawer and headed for the door. As she opened the door to walk through, she pressed the garage door opener, which allowed the sunlight to come pouring into the dark space.

Belle finished her work as she heard the sound of the truck firing up in the garage. She stood from the office chair and moved aside to push it forward before grabbing her purse and headed for the garage.

## Chapter 8

# Eternity Before Time

Anxious to get started, Jessica woke early and got ready for her day. She stood in front of her desk and carefully pulled the scroll from its protective case. She pulled the end of the scroll, easing the top roll away from herself on the desk. She noticed right away that this time the scroll was right side up. Looking at the top of the parchment she sat down to begin deciphering the words. Several reference books were nearby, and she began to write the words and meanings together on a yellow legal pad, gathering a sense of what the words meant as well as the nuances of the meanings.

Once she had a clear understanding from what she would call a "section" of the text, she began her interpretation into a readable rendition in English. And so it began...

---

*Pondering all of existence,*
*He had only to consider Himself.*

He was alone. He had no mother, no father. He had no expectation of seeing anyone, certainly no one like himself.

There had been no beginning, no ending. No expanse of time, no concept of time. Nothing had started; all was as it was. This paradigm was about to change. Change itself had never been; there had never been a cause for change. There was no need for anything and no desire for anything.

This one existed in perfect completeness, lacking nothing.

Nothing else existed. No substance, no concept, no idea, no parameters, no forms of measurement and nothing to measure. Other than the One, there was nothing. Absolutely nothing.

His next action would change His life for all eternity.

In the beginning, Elohim created...

Elohim, complete in every way, began to be restless. The entire essence of this One shuddered as turbulent forces moved within. Desire, something never felt before, bubbling up from the recesses of Elohim until it reached the place it could be expressed.

The Word came forth, "Companion."

Spoken thought became a new expression of Elohim's essence. This form of expression came to be know as "The Word". This uncreated expression of Himself was not separate from Elohim, but instead more of a branch of His existence.

After a short pause The Word came forth again, "It is not good for Elohim to be alone." This One, though complete in every way, desired another. This concept of aloneness or the desire for companionship had never been thought of before and this one thought would change everything.

Wisdom quickened within Him, this puzzle must be solved, this desire must be fulfilled. Something entirely new was taking place in the One, and once expressed, this desire had to be realized. Once the desired outcome became fully known, every possible way to achieve the desire was explored at once, with the one clear solution instantly evident and the steps to get there laid out. One by one, many millions of steps appeared in an instant. Something had begun from the end to the beginning.

The solution, though something completely unthought of before, would come through something else brand new. Something separate from Elohim, something distinct and yet like Him. There was nothing "other" than Elohim so this "one" must be in Him and would have to come out, to be separated. A division had to be made. Elohim would need to remove a small portion. This portion would need to have its own life and be distinct from Himself.

Once separate, this "one" would need to be allowed to grow and develop independent of Himself, to branch out, finding new aspects of itself, realizing who and what it was, and for what purpose it was made. It would need to have a life of its own; after all, this helper could not come to Him without first being separate and apart from Him.

This "other" would eventually seek to be with Elohim and would be weaker yet equal to Him. This one would be the completion of the desire of Elohim. A counterpart or bride.

A bride cannot just be built; it cannot be created outright. It must be formed. Forming takes perseverance, patience, "Love."

There it was, The Word expressed it. Elohim had felt this branch forming and the sheer emotion became a driving force coming forth. Love. Wisdom pondered the depths of love and could see in an instant the incredible ecstasy on one side and an equally incredible cost on the other. At once, knowing the cost, The Word shouted, "I will pay this cost! My counterpart is worth it!"

## Chapter 9

# Day One

### The Foundations of Choice

*In the beginning Elohim created the heavens and the Earth.*

*And the Earth came to be formless and empty and darkness was on the face the deep. And the Spirit of Elohim was moving on the face of the waters.*

*And Elohim said, "Let light come to be," and light came to be.*

*And Elohim saw the light, that it was good. And Elohim separated the light from the darkness.*

*And Elohim called the light 'day' and the darkness He called 'night'. And there came to be evening and morning, the first day.*

_____

Travail, the One's entire being trembled under the exertion of this new work. The bounds of time not yet grasping nor able to calculate the profound effort of the One's labor. This meticulous endeavor caused an anticipation to rise within the One. The work continued until everything was complete, down to the most finite detail. Once creation was ready and formed within the One, it moved as if pushed in steadily building contractions to the surface. Only now, unlike the Word, it did not form a branch. Instead, with the last and most fervent contraction creation was born. Smaller than an electron, all that would ever be made now existed, separate and distinct from the One. This seed had been created knowing the end from the beginning, every event planned for, every decision made outside of the One, accounted for. Every possibility would lead to one end. This beginning could have but one conclusion.

And The Word commanded the seed of creation, "Be fruitful and multiply!"

The seed, so small and insignificant, began to tremble under the influence of the spoken words. A crack appeared on it's surface. Stillness overtook the embodiment of all things created. All at once it split open, shock waves propelling all that was within, in an explosive rush. Progression, the first of a new occurrence, something happening in a sequence, not all at once. Something measurable was happening, which in turn brought forth something else entirely new-the birth of time, the relentless chronologer. Never stopping, never resting, its measuring only slowed by the speeds this massive explosion made possible. The multiverse aged at a steady rate while the fast moving particles aged much more slowly. The relativistic nature of time evident. At the same instant, the birth of dimensions, nearly one hundred, began unfolding, collapsing and splitting apart. Many collapsed within milliseconds of birth, their purpose fulfilled. Other dimensions, split from each other, dividing into three distinct groupings. Each group of dimensions forming a unique cosmos. Three of these cosmoses or universes began simultaneously forming the multiverse. The three expansions, consisting of Paradise, Cosmos, and Crypsis, pushed forward. Never before had anything been seen. Never before had anyone seen. Elohim saw these ever expanding macrocosms of fractal energy beginning to form matter. The multidimensional multiverses had begun expanding in all directions, creating space as they grew.

———————

There was a knock at the door. Belle was in the kitchen and looked out the window toward the front door to see who was there.

"Jessica, it's Dr. Angelo!"

"Really?"

"Yep, I'll get the door."

Belle ran her hands through her hair before pulling the the door open.

"Dr. Angelo! It's good to see you."

Michael bowed, "I'm glad to see you as well, Isabella, please call me Michael."

"All right, Michael, won't you come in? Jessica has been working hard all morning."

"Good! I'm glad the project is underway." Michael stepped into the entryway of the home, ducking slightly as he passed the door frame. The ceiling inside was much higher than Jessica's office ceiling.

Jessica reached the entry way in time to see Michael looking up at the ceiling. "Michael! Welcome to our summer vacation spot!"

Michael bowed slightly toward Jessica, "I hear you are making progress, I am glad for that."

Jessica reached out for Michael's hand and pulled him into the family room.

"Jessica, I cannot stay. I am here to see that you two are settled and check on your progress. I see you have begun."

"Yes, I have, although I have to say, that first chapter is rather cryptic."

"Well, do the best you can. You are trying to describe things that defy reason in the world you currently live in. Just stick with it, I am sure you are up to the task."

"Thanks for the vote of confidence."

Michael continued, "The second reason I came today was to let you know that you need to keep this project secret. You will be asked about it, people might be curious about newcomers in this area, and you need to keep the specifics of this project to yourselves. Do you understand?"

Jessica spoke up first, "Yeah, we'll keep it secret, right Belle?"

"Yeah, sure. Novelists almost never share what their books are about anyway. No sweat."

Michael nodded his head "OK, good, I have to go. Keep at it, and I will drop in from time to time."

Michael headed for the door.

———————

In the darkness of the newly created space, atoms began to converge, forming the first molecules. These molecules came together forming the elements: iron, copper, manganese, zinc, and many others. Metals, gases, and salts, combining to form rock, dirt, and water. The elements gathered together forming a growing number of expanding spherical balls of solid rock or gas, all of this somehow orchestrated.

The gathering chunks of rock began to experience another created force-gravity-and with it as their sizes increased, the pressures throughout the rocks began to form spherical shapes, the most efficient shape when a single force is pulling from a common center. As they grew in size, so grew their gravitational pull. They began behaving like giant vacuums in space, collecting any and all of the gases and debris within the reach of the new gathering force.

This gravity worked within the expansion, all mass drawing all other masses to itself. The forces diminishing exponentially with distance. The original explosive forces worked opposite the gravitational forces. The explosive forces prevailed on the larger scale, while gravity prevailed on the smaller scale.

Throughout the expanding space, through the billions of forming spherical rocks and gas giants, rotation began. Maelstroms began forming throughout the multiverse, tiny, solar system sized. As the rocky planets orbited about their large central gaseous brother, huge gaseous spheres formed at the center of each maelstrom. These central bodies were fully ten times the size of any neighboring sphere. Each body throughout the universe began to spin on its own center, revolving. A tiny percentage of the spheres began spinning in an opposite direction as compared to the others.

These systems acted as small parts of much larger maelstroms and revolved around the most dense of the bodies in space, the dark cores. These bodies began burning; however, their gravity was so strong that even the light from their own fires could not escape. Thus creation remained dark. Trillions of smaller systems rotated around these black cores, forming galaxies, billions of them. All of this taking a long or short time, depending upon where the measurement was taken.

In one small portion of this new universe, tucked away in one of many similar galaxies, a sphere of rock began to assemble. As the rock grew to thousands of miles in diameter, the pressures in the center increased. Gravity produced by the massive body began pulling everything within range toward itself. Other elements condensed from the surrounding space to form water on the surface. The amount of water produced on this particular body was enormous, much more than its neighboring planets. The density of the water exerted even more pressure downward until the rocky core began to glow in the tremendous pressure induced heat. The fluidity of the liquid rock allowed the heavier elements to sink to the center forming a pliable core of molten iron. The center of the Earth was now alive and churning, the crushing forces produced heat that flowed back up throughout the newly formed water covered planet.

Barely noticeable in the darkness, a vapor surrounded and permeated the water. This entity, difficult to see, moved in fractal waves, seemingly without any kind of order or goal. Yet, it continued it's relentless work even as...

A thunderous voice, echoing through all of space and time called out, "Let light come to be!"

At the very moment these words ended, creation responded in kind. A great flash of white light, filled all of space, then the thunder of this incredible response, both majestic and terrible boomed and crackled, shaking the very planet Elohim had just assembled. Cracks formed in the rock crust under the waves. As the light ushered forth incredible heat and the surface waters responded almost immediately, evaporation created a mist. The atmospheric cycle had begun.

---

*And Elohim saw the light, that it was good. And Elohim separated the light from the darkness.*

---

The light, obeying the very will of the creator began to separate, leaving in it's wake the thick, inky darkness that had been there before, until it lit only a slowly shrinking portion of the Earth. The nebulas light collected and drew down toward the large central body.

The light moved, disappearing from the Crypsis until only darkness remained, shrinking back into Paradise, while the light and darkness were both allowed to remain in the Earth region.

The kingdom of light and the kingdom of darkness had been established. The earth placed in a tension between the two. Now choice could be made. The foundation was established.

---

The great sea at the foot of the throne-chariot, calm and restful, smooth as glass, began to stir. The ground began shaking as the water became a great boiling mass. Wisps of fire appeared on the surface of the churning water, the flames spread and split apart until the surface was filled with individual fires of varying shapes and sizes. Each fire began to breathe as life entered them.

Metatron, the scribe, a tall, slender being wearing a dingy gray tunic, seated in the corner of the throne room rose, placed his quill pen into the ink vat, and rose to his feet. Making his way to the edge of the great sea, opposite the throne-chariot. His eyes sparkled as he motioned for one of the larger flames to come toward him.

The flame moved as directed, if cautiously from the water's surface. The bottom of the flame mass split into four great pillars of flame, the body above the flaming pillars spread out to form tail, neck, and head. A thin membrane began covering this creature. As it spread, dozens of layers of red skin flowed over the first, one after the other, forming a tough, porous hide inlaid with fine gem stones. These stones were not only in the skin but were windows into this creature, each stone showing the brilliant light from the fire within. Beams of light shown from the creature, split by the many facets of each stone.

As the skin formed over this being, its powerful build could be seen more fully. Under it's skin, musculature began to form, pushing out on the skin that in turn revealed the striations in the lean muscle mass. The toes ended, and large hooked talons grew out, serrated horns pushing up and out the end of the creature's powerful tail, as sharp as fractured obsidian. His head and neck rimmed with horns and his large mouth filled with white razor sharp teeth, fangs, and a tongue split at the end, forming a fork. Just as the new creature gained the ability to speak, it erupted into glorious song in multiple harmonies, praises to it's creator, it's voice filling the air with majestic music.

The scribe approached the massive fiery serpent, his long white hair blended with his white beard. He reached up to place his hand on the beasts shoulder and said, "You are Lucifer, Light Bearer, the bright and morning star. Your kind is called Seraphim." Metatron's head bowed, just for a moment, as though he were listening to something. He lifted his head and motioned for Lucifer to move forward. Metatron looked back to the sea, his flaming blue eyes showing the slightest hint of a smile. Lifting his arms toward the sea he beckoned to the flames, "Seraphim! Come forth!"

At once, millions of large flames moved toward him, emerging from the water, skin and jewels began covering them just as they had with Lucifer. These seraphim serpents numbered over one hundred and thirty million. Each as individual as the flicker of a flame. As they left the sea each moved forward even as their skin formed, allowing those behind to also emerge. Each joining with Lucifer in praising the Creator. The glorious voices in the throne room rose as the new seraphim serpents heard and quickly learned the song Lucifer was singing. The voices blended with the fierce thunder strikes from the throne, the thunder acting as percussion to the magnificent joy filled song.

Smaller flames were still in the sea, the waters beneath them bubbling and churning. Metatron, his eyes staring at the throne, nodded and looked to the flames in the sea and called out, "Archangels, come forth!"

Seven tall and slender flames emerged from the water, skin forming to cover each like the creatures before them only this time the skin was thin and delicate, not heavy and thick like the seraphim before them. Tall, gracefully flowing flames on top of their heads began to separate, forming strands that continued to wave in the air, changing color to various shades, then settled and formed long shining hair. Their eyes formed the same as the Dragons' eyes and ornaments, looking like translucent jewels revealing the fire within them.

Metatron brought a stack of seven garments, walked to the first of these new beings, and handed him a robe saying, "You are Remiel, the Thunder of the Creator." Remiel opened the tunic and put it on, while Metatron walked to the next and much larger angel saying, "and you are Zarachiel, the Command of the Creator." Zarachiel received his tunic, and Metatron continued on to the next.

"You are Raguel, the Friend of the Creator," and to the next "You are Raphael, Angel of Healing." Metatron handed Raphael his tunic as he turned to the next archangel and said, "You are Uriel, Archangel of Fire, you need no tunic. Uriel nodded, his entire body a brilliant orange flame. Metatron continued to the next angel, "You are Gabriel, the Messenger of the Creator," handing Gabriel his tunic. Then turning to the last Archangel, Metatron said, "and you, you are called Michael, the Viceroy of the Creator," Michael took his tunic and bowed his head to the scribe.

"Archangels, you are of the kind, Cherubim." Then walking back to the sea, Metatron held out his arms and called out, "Cherubim come forth!"

More than two hundred and sixty million flames began making their way to the edge of the water, proceeding out onto the dry stone floor. Again, skin and jeweled eyes began forming, as it had with the Archangels.

Metatron called to the archangels, "Archangels, please give me some help passing out tunics," as he motioned to a giant store room full of garments at the edge of the throne room. The robes were organized into six areas for the newly forming angels, with the exception of the fiery ones, to come and receive their garments.

———————

And Elohim called the light 'day' and the darkness He called 'night'. And there came to be evening and there came to be morning, the first day.

## Chapter 10

# Day Two

*And Elohim said, "Let an expanse come to be in the midst of the waters and let it separate the waters from the waters."*

*And Elohim made the expanse and separated the waters which were under the expanse from the waters which were above the expanse. And it came to be so.*

*And Elohim called the expanse 'heavens.' And there came to be evening and there came to be morning, the second day.*

---

The meeting had gone as planned, Lucifer had called together all of his generals and the archangels. He wanted to be sure everyone understood the directive He had received from the Creator, what was

ْ ,ected of them and the importance of carrying out the directive correctly. They all felt the weight of his words when he had finished by saying, "We have one chance to get this right, there are *no* second chances!"

―――――――

Metatron walked to the edge of the balcony, hundreds of feet in the air, he peered out over the miles of green grass before him, the lush forest as its backdrop with massive trees, low lying bushes and wild flowers with an endless array of living colors that swayed in the ebb and flow of the Spirit of Elohim. Below him and running to the right and left of the balcony was a main street, made of a very common element, at least common here, gold so pure that the ground beneath it could be seen. This street, fully five feet thick and perfectly flat, with no seams to reveal how it was made. He looked down the yellow path to the right. There were elegant wild rose hedges of every color and variety interspersed with flaming oil-producing shrubs.

The balcony he stood on was part of the temple. This building made from living stone and ever growing trees moved constantly. Gently swaying this way or that, the barely perceptible movement revealed the continual growth. The outside of the building lined with massive redwood trees formed columns around the entire perimeter. Between the grand redwoods stood olive trees bearing fruit always in season. Mature when created, these living buildings and trees would continue their slow growth forever.

The temple had many rooms surrounding one large meeting hall, canopied by an enormous domed ceiling, made from polished titanium with an arch and web structure, seemingly made from one solid piece, each opening in the complex framework filled with the finest silver. Grand columns along the interior curved walls created as living granite, very much like the redwood trees outside the building, each tying into the ceiling supports with stoney branches, some of which seemed to coil around the titanium webbing of the ceiling, others reaching to the branches of neighboring columns binding them together. The focus of the room was a 777' tall wheeled throne-chariot, made from a thick sapphire crystal. The organic structure of this stone formed into webbing and, like everything else in this place, had life and breath. While the seat and back remained perfectly still, the other structures moved and flowed, as though the state of the stone remained slightly liquid and uncrystallized, forming new supports while retracting old ones. The throne was in a state of constant newness. Magnificent gold and silver accents, while amazingly intricate, remained undefinable, moving and changing from one design to another, never repeating any pattern.

Surrounding the blazing wheels of the throne-chariot were the Ophanim orbs resembling wheels within wheels, somehow. These Ophanim were able to move and turn to travel in any direction at will. Usually unseen, the number of these beings were vast, greatly outnumbering the Seraphim and Cherubim combined. Several thousand could be seen in the throne room at any given time. These rulers of the celestial bodies governed the paths and forces that dominate the universe-that is, the stars, planets, comets, asteroids, dark matter, and dark energy. The Ophanim flew so fast around the throne that their fiery trails resembled the paths of planets within the planetary systems with the throne being their central fiery star.

From beneath the throne flowed a crystal clear river winding back and forth on the floor. The great volume continually seeking the parts of the floor willing to allow its current. So flowed the outpouring, moving this way and that, then ending in a water fall that dropped downward into a crystalline sea, separating the throne from the main hall. On either side of the throne were bridges, one on each side, spanning the sea in high arches of pure white and yet semitransparent in appearance.

Above the throne a storm lingered, a noisy green swirling vortex circling at great speed produced massive lightning strikes and the noisy crackling and booming of thunder. The lightning branched into dozens of bright fingers searching the floor, then disappearing. Smoke rose into the air from wherever the lightning or its fingers had either burned through the air or touched down. The charred floor quickly healed from the powerful bursts of energy.

To the left of the throne, was another smaller chair, made identical to the first. It was a curious site. This throne represented a mystery the Creator had not explained to him. He had no idea who or what would sit in this seat. Similar in size to the throne to the right and surrounding the central throne-chariot were 24 thrones. These were pure white marble, each with individual markings, making each different and unique. These thrones were static, a very unusual trait in this place. The thrones had very specific markings, no movement. Each had a look similar to the main thrones, at least in their organic nature, yet each remained still. *Why would anything be made without life in it?*

Looking past the 24 thrones and encompassing all the thrones stood a stadium, made of pure white marble. The stands could easily hold several billion individuals and were clearly made for beings of the same size as those who would use the smaller thrones. Whoever would be sitting here would be very small. The stadium opened in the front, facing the rest of the great hall. Like the 24 chairs this great stadium remained motionless.

Descending the stairs from the balcony to the floor Metatron peered out to the great hall and wondered at how much larger this place looked without the host of paradise, since they had risen out of the very sea before him, and the entire angelic group had once stood in the great hall he now crossed.

On the throne sat Metatron's Creator. Revealing Himself in this place as a massive and continuous towering flame, violently raging and enveloped in an ever-moving cloud of steam and smoke that expanded from the flames and dissipated in a continual discharge. This One from Whom all power emanated would ever remain inexhaustible. He thought to himself that it was little wonder that this One's name was Elohim, a word that would forever refuse clear definition.

Metatron had reached the edge of the water. Across the sea he could see the fiery stones, each with different colored flames, and the seven gold lamp stands, each with seven flames whose fires burned bright and tall.

Watching the cloud, his eyes were drawn to the fire, and he found himself gazing into the terrifying heart of fire and water.

Hands folded in front of him, Metatron began rising into the air. Eyes staring into the flames, he began to see a vision of an individual with great white wings, his shoulders slumped. His body turned away as he gazed upon gold armor which was leaning in the corner of a room. The angel turned, revealing his face. Michael, now with magnificent wings turned, revealing his own armor, deeply gashed, his skin clearly seen to have ugly scars beneath the torn metal. A bereaved expression covered his face beneath the weariness. His eyes vacant.

Metatron's brow furrowed and he asked out loud, "What has happened?" He had no words to express the overwhelming sadness he saw in the face of this, the last archangel created. His heart grew heavy and he asked the Creator, "What are you showing me?"

"I'm showing you what will surely happen, when Michael is victorious."

"He doesn't look victorious, he looks sad."

"I show you the face of one who does not harden his heart to me. The victory he will see must take place, as there is another who's heart has begun to be cynical of my motives, to judge me. This one's heart is hardening against me and my ways, and it is this condition that will cause paradise itself to suffer loss. Through it all, Michael will rise and be victorious. However, victory cannot come without loss.

'The events leading up to this vision I've shown you must now take place, and you must record the truth of the matter, you must write from my perspective, my story will be given to you, and you will write it faithfully, I trust you because your heart has already proven to be true. You have already chosen and you can be trusted with my words."

Metatron stood for a moment, trying to process what he had seen while recounting the task the Creator had just charged him with, "These mysteries are beyond my comprehension, how can I hope to write from your perspective? My eyes do not see things as your eyes do."

"I will cause your eyes to remain open, your ears to hear me and my ways, and your heart to remain soft. The answers are never found in you, it is not for you to trust your eyes to see as I see, but to trust that I give you vision. As you rely on my vision you will see as I see, as you rely on my voice, you will hear my Word, and as you trust me with all that you are, you will have my ways within you. It is not for you to understand, but to experience my mysteries."

"You honor me, and I am forever thankful." Metatron said.

"You honor Me, and that honor will continually renew you." Elohim said.

---

Belle turned the truck into the small Starbucks parking lot. The lot was full and a Jeep was just backing out of a parking space at the front of the store. She waited for the Jeep to exit and pulled the truck into the spot where the Jeep had been, another vehicle entered the parking lot behind her. She had spent the morning grocery shopping and thought it would be a good idea to get herself and Jessica a nice vanilla latte.

She entered the small coffee shop to find a line of half a dozen people waiting to order. She took her place behind them and read over the familiar menu.

An older woman entered the shop. She had long grey hair, parted down the middle. No bangs, no frills, just combed straight down to the sides. It looked frizzed and brittle, probably a common thing here, being so dry.

Belle turned back to the front counter, only four more customers to go before she could order. She felt a chill and looked to see if the front door was open. It wasn't, and besides, it was a warm day today. She crossed her arms and looked up to see if she had moved under a vent or something.

"It's a nice day isn't it?" The question startled Belle just a little.

Belle turned to see the older woman behind her, staring out the plate glass windows toward Pike's Peak. "Yes, it's a lovely day, if a little cool."

"Oh honey, this isn't cool, this is warm, must be seventy degrees or so today. You know it only get's to eighty for a few days in August up here."

"Oh wow, I had no idea."

"You must be new."

"Yep. Been here a just a couple of weeks now."

"We don't get many young people up here. Are you working at the Walmart?"

"No, my boss and I moved here for the summer. She's a college professor, and I edit for her."

The stranger turned to look directly at Belle. "Oh that's great, what are you editing?"

Belle glanced at the woman before looking back toward the mountain. "It's a novel. That's all I can really say."

The woman's stare remained, and a smile crept onto her face. "Oh come now, you can give a little hint, can't you? I won't tell anyone."

Belle smiled curtly, "I'm sorry, I really can't say anything."

"Well, you can say what type of novel it is."

"I really can't, I'm sorry. May I ask you a question, though?"

This seemed to throw the stranger off guard. "Umm, of course, honey."

"OK, is there a good Mexican restaurant up here?"

"As a matter of fact there are two, if you can believe that, being such a small town."

"Where are they? We go out to eat now and then, and I'd love to be able to suggest one."

"Let's see, there's Casa Grande, and Fiesta Mexicana."

"Oh I've seen the Fiesta one."

"OK, then the other one is Casa Grande and it's down highway 24, you'll pass the Walgreens, it's off the road a bit on the left. If you get to the Swiss Chalet, you've gone too far."

"OK, I appreciate that." Only one person was between Belle and the counter. She hoped the stranger wouldn't bring up the...

"You're sure you can't tell me anything about the book?"

Belle again felt the stare of this woman, a cold chill ran down her spine. "I'm sorry ma'am, I really can't. Not if I want to keep my job!" Belle laughed a bit trying to ease the tension.

"Fair enough. We get writers up here from time to time. Secretive bunch, that one." The stranger's eyes remained fixed.

Belle felt as though the stranger's very will was boring into her. "Yes Ma'am. Very much so."

At last a welcome voice was directed at the younger woman, "Miss, may I take your order?"

Belle moved forward to order her drinks. "I'll have two grande vanilla latte's please."

Belle paid and stepped to the side, the cashier spoke to the older woman. "Good morning, ma'am, may I take your order?"

"Oh just a moment, I didn't look at the menu yet."

"That's all right, take your time."

Belle collected her drinks. "Nice to meet you ma'am, and thanks for the information."

"You're welcome, honey. Good luck with your project."

Belle thanked the woman and backed through the entrance before turning outside to leave.

The older woman watched Belle as she walked to the vehicle, placed both cups on the bed rail, and searched her purse for her keys. The woman behind the counter interrupted her thoughts, "Ma'am, have you decided?"

"You know, I don't think I want to order anything after all."

"OK, well let me know if you change your mind."

The older woman walked to the plate glass windows at the front of the store and watched the young editor back the truck out of the parking space.

Belle couldn't get the older woman's stare out of her mind. It was unnerving. She backed out of the parking space and as she moved the shift lever from reverse to drive, she glanced back toward the coffee shop. The older woman was staring at her, unflinching.

---

With only two days before the parade, the generals worked hard to organize the enormous practice fields for drill practice. The Creator wanted to see all the troops displayed before Him in an organized fashion and there was no time to waste. Once the choirs were organized, they would leave immediately for parade practice.

---

A giant grass field in Paradise buzzed with activity, each general working with his senior officers to get schedules in order, and organize this huge number of angels. All of the hundreds of millions of angels had gathered to be divided into their separate choirs. Uriel, was known as the "fire of Elohim" because he was completely ablaze, and his troops took on this same attribute. His troops were therefore easy to spot. As were the seraphim, again all being dragons of various size and color. The rest of the angelic choirs worked diligently to determine where they belonged and report for duty.

Of course the Seraphim and Uriel's choir were the first to achieve any sort of order and were the first to leave to their designated practice areas. They walked in large groups without any apparent order, this would change shortly.

One of the angels discovered that if his sword hit anything, it thundered. His face turned red at this realization as he picked it up off the ground. It had slipped from his hand as he pulled it from it's sheath. Others saw this, some laughing as he awkwardly bent over to pick it up. Then several realized the discovery that had just been made and tried out their swords. Thunder, if heard would send them running to the one known as the "thunder of Elohim," Remiel's section.

As the groups of angels left for their designated areas, organization became easier. Much of the symmetry they would need was achieved quickly, from proper spacing to marching in step. The minor touches were taking longer, from keeping in step to keeping their spacing correct. It all came down to concentration. In the end, looking at the troops marching in formation, each vast grouping took on the glow of its leader even more than when they were separate. It was an amazing accomplishment to organize so many angels so quickly.

---

Forming up in Remiel's section, one angel turned to the other asking, "Are ya gonna be able to hold on to that sword?"

"Yeah," he said, laughing nervously.

"I'm Tzadkiel" the first cherubim said still smiling.

"I'm Jeremiel," looking out over the huge number of cherubim, "I'm not sure how all these troops are going to be able to parade past the throne in one day, I mean, we don't walk *that* fast!" Jeremiel said under his breath, Tzadkiel agreed with a nod.

Another angel, looking past Tzadkiel offered a suggestion, "Maybe Elohim will stop time, then it doesn't matter *how* slow we are... My name is Raziel, good to meet you two."

Jeremiel introduced the two of them, "I'm Jeremiel and this is Tzadkiel, nice to meet you," Tzadkiel turned and nodded toward Raziel.

Just then, from the front of the choir was heard, "Angels, Attennnn-chun!" With that all eyes faced front with the sound of millions of angels coming to attention."

---

The Spirit of Elohim, still working in the waters, began lifting the outer layer of rock up away from the core, allowing the water above it to fill in under the spherical crust. Over a period of hours the outer layer of rock had formed a new crust surrounded above and beneath by mile-thick layers of water. Elohim's Spirit released the rock and allowed it to settle, having formed it into one piece.

## Chapter 11

# Sulphur

That smell, faint but disgusting nonetheless, made her face cringe and distracted her from her work with the scroll. Jessica looked around the room and wondered what could be causing the nauseating odor. There it was again, stronger than before.

*Maybe Belle knows what could be causing it,* she thought. "Belle?" No answer. *She must still be out running errands.*

Her vision began to change, everything around her seemed to come into sharper focus while the air, though still invisible, seemed to gain texture or weight, a fluid quality. Her vision almost made her forget about the scent. Something dark moved off to her right. The room's colors continued to shift to more vibrant hues. She began to feel dizzy. Every piece of furniture in the room seemed to be moving, while remaining still. Everything looked alive.

There, she could see something she hadn't seen before, a shadow in the corner opposite her desk. A shadow where the light from the window shone brightly. It swayed back and forth, when all was still outside and it had volume, somehow. No, it could not be a shadow. She sat motionless, as if she could hide simply by remaining still. Her vision shifted again, and now she could see two yellow orbs with a vertical slit in the center of each orb peering at her. She caught her breath. No more than 15 feet away and staring directly at her.

She whispered, "Michael... Michael, if you're near..." She thought she heard a muffled snicker from the darkness in the corner.

Her attention was suddenly diverted by a sound so intense that she almost jumped out of her chair. A gigantic boom immediately followed by crackling and distant thunder. The presence in the corner must have heard it too, for the eyes moved all around, then back to her. Her vision suddenly shifted once more, as if lenses before her eyes were changing rapidly. This time the walls of the study and the entire home became transparent. She clenched her eyelids tight with the thought that everything would be normal once she reopened them.

She was wrong. She could see beyond the walls of her home a battle taking place outside, perhaps 30 yards from where she sat. Alone in what had become a glass box, she watched a battle rage all around her.

There must have been a dozen or so dragon-like *things*, all shriveled up, horns sticking out everywhere, covered in scales with boney ridges running along their backs from head to tail. Some had spiked tails. Others had many horns on their heads poking out from every conceivable place. Still huge, some had both, yet all looked gaunt and undernourished.

These anorexic beasts moved in quick bursts of speed, fighting against maybe eight or nine winged warriors who looked very much like Michael when he first appeared to her on the beach. None looked exactly like him, some had dark skin and wings, others more pale. All the warriors had a light about them, an aura of dancing colors, barely perceptible.

The two sides battled, most of their movements faster than she could comprehend-the entire fight was a tangled blur of darkness and light. The dragons ripped at the angels with their claws, horns and teeth, while the angels fought using their shields and swords as both defensive and offensive weapons.

She saw a dragon lunging for an angel's throat, his face met with a shield, bashing him away. The angel's blue-flamed sword hacked through the serpent's side, sending a glowing fluid spurting into the air. The dragon leapt at the angel again, mouth wildly biting the air. Head butting the shield away, this time the serpent latched onto the angel's upper arm. The angel's head lifted in pain as one membranous wing covered the face while the dragon's talons dug into the skin on the angel's throat and back of the neck and head, savagely ripping and slashing with no mercy whatsoever. The dragon's tail swung around the angel's body in a blur as it impaled the angel in the back, penetrating through the armor with a loud thud. The angel's body arched forward, feet stumbled to keep a balance, sword and shield falling noisily to the ground as the angel dropped, hands contorted in pain. The dragon continued his clawing as his tail moved up and down, freeing itself while causing more internal damage to the warrior. A viscous substance, orange-red and glowing, spread down the monster's tail, steaming as it dripped in large globs on the ground.

The dragon's jaw worked in a sawing motion, the glowing fluid seeping through the dragon's teeth and down the angel's arm.

Jessica could see that the dragons were gaining the upper hand, and the fight was moving steadily toward her home, directly toward the very study where she sat. She heard the thunder claps and cracks again but now they were rapidly intensifying. The dragons appeared to become anxious; several stopped their assault to scan the skies, like terrified dogs looking for the source of the thunder.

In the distance, high in the air, a brightness caught her attention, growing as it moved closer and closer. Then it split apart becoming 50 or so smaller blue lights. The fiery beings moved like bullets aimed directly into the fray.

"No!" She screamed, fearing these new arrivals would doom the angels to further brutality.

The first of the fiery ones crashed into the dragon who was still sawing at the angel's arm, flinging it into the air. The dragon skillfully used its wings to right itself, landing on its hind feet, one of its front paws, or hands, held its side. Then the dragon recovered just in time to be pummeled again by a second fiery bullet.

The flaming angel shouldered into the dragon, lifting him into the air and hurling him against a massive fir tree. With a loud crack, the dragon's body hit hard, bending around the tree, flopped to the ground, lifeless.

"Yes!" She shouted.

The new arrivals continued their assault, diving in and disrupting individual fights, completely overcoming the gnarled dark dragons. One by one the injured beasts leapt into the air, and made quick retreats. One of the larger serpents flew to the one fallen by the tree, picked him up, and flew away.

When the final dragon had left, the fiery beings landed among the first group of angels. They moved to those most brutalized, pairing up next to them and checking injuries.

Jessica turned to look back into the corner of her study where the shadow remained. Only now, with her vision clearer, she could plainly see the man-sized dragon staring at her. The tail coiled around the body, wings folded down, and the neck formed an "s" as if it were a rattlesnake ready to strike. Fumes of yellow vapor slowly oozed from its nose. The same cold chill continued down her spine, and she couldn't help but let out a terrified yet muted whimper. Something about the dragon's posture let her know he was enjoying her fear.

Jessica rose to her feet and as she did so, the dragon in the corner reared back, as if frightened. She was astounded. Why would this terrifying creature, who seemed to relish her fear only moments ago, now appear to be afraid of her?

Then she saw the dragon's eyes move steadily upward. She became aware of another presence, a *large* presence, behind her. She turned slowly to her left and could see a large brown-feathered wing and an angelic warrior wearing a silver breastplate that covered a white garment, and an immensely tall shield strapped to his back. She looked up at the angel's face, whose eyes never left the intruder in the corner. Ripples emanated from this angel where the ceiling used to be, or still was, though now unseen.

She turned her head to the right and saw a large sword burning with blue flames. She quickly stumbled to the left to remove herself from the path between these two. The large angel swayed backwards, knees and hips flexing, before springing across the room, shooting right through her desk, catching the dragon by a hind leg as it attempted a quick escape.

Lunging back, the dragon clamped down on the angel's big forearm only to have its head clubbed by the hilt of the angel's sword. The angel sheathed the weapon and with the right arm grabbed the neck of the dragon. Face winced with pain, the angel ripped the dragon's teeth from his arm. The serpent now flopped around loosely as if dead or unconscious. The angel wiped his arm with his tunic and mopped up the glowing fluid. Jessica could only imagine it was angel blood, though it looked more like molten lava.

One of the fiery angels, walked toward the room, entering through the wall. The air where the wall was formerly visible shimmered with radiating waves as the angel moved through it.

"One got through?" the blazing angel asked.

The first angel looked up with disgust on his face. "The little ones can be real nuisances."

"What about *her*?"

"Her senses are awakened for the time being, she can see us. She seems to be all right, at least physically."

"We must not have any contact until Michael arrives."

The two moved back out to the others, the transparent wall reacting again as they passed. They reached the others as a much larger angel arrived, this one standing a full head taller than the angel carrying the small dragon. As this newcomer's light faded, the proportions transformed themselves, skin turning olive, hair almost black. The gold breastplate and armor melded into a black trench coat, jeans, and boots of a sort Jessica had seen before.

It was Michael.

He proceeded to converse for several minutes with several of the original angels. He moved among the injured and spoke with one of the fiery beings who looked to be in charge. He kept nodding as he listened. Finally he spoke and turned in the direction of the two angels that had just left Jessica's study. The fiery being called out to the others who lifted many of the injured and flew away, two carrying each injured one.

Michael stood with the two angels who had been in her study, listened as the one holding the serpent spoke. A look of concern spread across the Archangel's face. Then he turned to look toward the study. The one holding the dragon continued talking, gesturing with his arms, flinging the little dragon like a forgotten rag doll. Michael listened and nodded. There was a pause after the angel stopped talking, then Michael slowly began walking to the study, the two followed along. The three moved through the wall, the same shimmering occurred once again. This time the effect was much larger, revealing the shapes of windows and picture frames as the ripples spread and dissipated. The three stood looking at Jessica.

Michael still looked concerned when he spoke. "Jessica, something has happened here today, your senses have been awakened."

Her whole body trembled as she moved back behind her desk, easing down onto the cushion of her chair and looking like a scared little girl.

"I've never seen anything like this, what has happened to me, how is it that I can see through the house?" " she stammered, trembling. Then, her voice firmer, she asked, "Are those angels going to be all right?"

Michael's burning eyes softened, *She's concerned for our kind*. "Elohim has decided to show you what is happening around you. I do not know how long this will last, and I know it must be frightening to get part of your original sight back. As you can now see, there are many of our kind here to help protect you." Then he looked around the room, "And yet this small intruder got through."

The angel holding the serpent pointed to the corner where the dragon had been. "It was over here, Sir." Michael moved to where the creature had been crouching.

The walls and ceiling were only visible when the angels interrupted their edges, sending ripples along the formerly solid surfaces. The Archangel looked human, and while his height in this form made him shorter than the eight-foot ceiling, his two companions were much taller. Ripples undulated around their necks and shoulders as they moved.

Michael continued, "The creature was sent to distract you; however, Elohim turned that plan around and has worked it for your benefit."

Jessica was puzzled, "For my good? What do you mean?"

"He has shown you how vital your mission is, how important it is for the enemy to disrupt you. A long time has passed since we have witnessed an attack as brazen as this. I will be posting more angels to your care."

Jessica leaned forward, head in hands. "I'm feeling really dizzy again." She reached for the edge of her desk to steady herself. "My eyes are hurting."

Michael nodded, "Your vision is fading. I will introduce my two compatriots to you while you can still see them. This one is Tzadkiel."

Tzadkiel bowed, holding the dragon behind his back.

Michael pointed toward the fire angel, "And over here is Kalil."

Bowing, Kalil spoke, "Now we meet formally. It is an honor to be of assistance in the service of Elohim."

"Thank you. Are the others out there going to be all right?"

Kalil nodded, "Once we return them to paradise they will be fine." He bowed again as he turned to leave, followed closely by Tzadkiel, still dragging the serpent behind him.

"Do not free him yet, Tzadkiel," Michael instructed.

Tzadkiel gave a knowing nod, "Understood."

"I will follow you in a moment..." Michael's voice trailed off.

Her vision began changing again, this time the new details began to blur and soften. The walls of her study became solid once again. She was able to see the wisp that was Tzadkiel move through the wall as her vision returned to normal.

She sat in her study with Michael. Her head hurt and she had many questions, yet her mind was so cluttered from all that had happened, she couldn't think clearly enough to ask a single one.

Michael asked, "Tell me what you remember, what stopped your work?"

"My eyes began to shift...no that wasn't it, wait, it was an odor. Like rotten eggs."

"Sulphur..." Michael nodded. "That traitor was sent to distract you. Elohim wanted you to see that."

"What do you mean?"

"You stopped working because you smelled sulphur. The villain must have been standing right next to you. All he had to do was breath on you, and you stopped working. Once your eyes started to see, he must have realized what was happening and moved to the corner. He may have hoped to scare you. The others outside were a diversion for the guardians."

"The fight outside was a diversion? I've never seen anything like that."

"As battles go, that was a small skirmish. I rejoice that Uriel was able to spare a few troops. And yes, it was a diversionary attack to let the small dragon slip in without being noticed... I am unaware how much you saw, but I know what seeing into our realm has done to others in the past. It is extremely rare for your kind to see reality. It was useful for you to see it, but should we not be focusing on one small lesson?"

"What lesson?"

"The enemy wants to stop you from completing your assignment, whatever it is. He will use whatever he can to accomplish that goal, even something as insignificant as a smell. This worked, and he knows it worked. He will keep sending attacks."

She shook her head, thinking, *What can I do to stop this?*

"Nothing," the Archangel answered, reading her thoughts. "He is relentless, he will continue to send attacks. You must be relentless as well, *more so.*"

He moved closer to the wall, toward the troops outside, "But know, as you've now seen, we are here helping more than you ever imagine. If you will excuse me." He bowed before slipping out of sight.

She sat silently for several minutes trying to make some sense of all she had seen. *I was distracted by so little.*

Determination flooded through her. She pivoted her chair back to the desk and resumed her work.

Beyond the walls, solid now, Michael addressed the angels, "Let us establish a new perimeter. Seventy-seven angels are required."

Michael turned his attention back to the study, peering through the wall to watch Jessica as she worked. He nodded his head. *You hold up your end of the bargain, and we will hold up ours.*

## Chapter 12

# Day Three

*And Elohim said, "Let the waters under the heavens be gathered together into one place and let dry land appear." And it came to be.*

---

As the newly-formed crust under the water began to move and settle, certain areas of the rock were laden with heavy minerals. Other areas were relatively light. As the heavy portions began to sink, the lighter portions were forced upward by the trapped water beneath the crust. Terrific forces were exerted on the ten-mile thick crust, causing it to bend, twist, and contort. The heavier sinking portions caused the lighter portions eventually to rise out of the water. These higher places separated the surface waters. The lowest points of this crust resembled rough pillars and rested on the outer core beneath it, supporting massive amounts of weight, their strength reinforced by the trapped water, now under very high pressure, surrounding them. These pillars became known as the pillars of fire, because the amazing pressures caused the bottoms of the pillars to glow red hot.

---

The largest single group of angels belonged to Lucifer. His keen sense of purpose and desire to excel pushed him forward into the challenge. Developing unity in such a large group would be a task, yet he knew he could do it. From the seraphim ranks he appointed nine generals answerable only to himself. Still, having the largest group, both in number and the size of the individuals, required he have the largest area in which to work.

Lucifer made his way to General Azazel, his most strategically-minded leader. "How are they doing?"

"Very well, Sir," the General said with a crisp salute. "Only minor matters to clean up, and they will be ready for tomorrow".

"Good." Lucifer turned to look down the row of generals, each either watching the progress of his group or talking with subordinates.

"All the others are making similar progress. We will be ready," Azazel assured his commander.

Lucifer nodded, thanked his general, and moved away. He did not want to distract Azazel from the task at hand. *He is someone I can count on,* the commander mused.

Azazel turned back to his officers, offered suggestions, and listened to progress reports.

---

*And Elohim called the dry land 'Earth,' and the collection of waters He called 'seas.' And Elohim saw that it was good.*

———————

With one day left to prepare, the troops appeared in good shape. After all, they just needed to be able to march past the throne in step. Other than Uriel's troops, whose flames blurred their appearance, it was easy to tell the troops were understanding the finer details of marching and staying in unison. Of course, there were the individuals who started with the wrong foot, then had to shuffle to get into step, but the realization that rested on them all was that Elohim the Creator would be present at the parade, and this fact meant their concentration level was high.

Michael had no doubt the cherubim would be ready on time and had assured Lucifer of this earlier in the day.

———————

Kalil and his new friends were making visible progress. They had not tripped or fallen in some time. The steady regimen of practice continued. In Paradise, night or darkness do not exist. The light of Elohim is ever-shining. That, and the fact that angels have no need for sleep, nor to eat, at least in the way humans think of eating, meant breaks could be kept at a minimum, and gains could be made quickly.

Kalil and the others in his group were the fire angels, completely consumed and burning at all times. All the angels were made from fire and water; however, with these it was obvious. The leadership had just dismissed the ranks to take a short break and Kalil, Hillel, and Malkiel were standing together, talking and stretching.

Kalil spoke first, "I think it is going well, don't you agree?" Kalil asked the others.

"I am still nervous," Hillel admitted. "We are going to be marching for the King to review us, and someone mentioned a surprise."

"What sort of surprise?"

A booming voice spoke from behind them, "We are going to give a small demonstration during the parade, a kind of a salute." This angel who spoke towered above them, and his bluer flame showed that he burned several hundred degrees hotter than they did, "All the choirs will be offering a salute. I overheard one of the generals talking about it." With that, he turned and walked away.

Malkiel called out to him, "Thank you!" and turned back to his friends. "Who was that?"

Kalil crossed his arms, "That was Ozel, an awesome being, would you not agree? Apparently, he had a short talk with Uriel, and not long after that his flame began to turn more blue."

Hillel began running back to the field and waving to the others, "Come on, they are forming back up!"

The other two, turned and followed Hillel back to their positions.

---

Movement continued in the crust until the highest parts had displaced most of the water and formed small mountains, large plateaus, and lakes, while revealing a large ocean that covered one-quarter of the planet's surface. Most of the water was now under the large land mass, in subterranean chambers.

---

*And Elohim said, "Let the Earth bring forth grass, the plant that yields seed and the fruit tree that yields fruit according to its kind, whose seed is in itself, on the Earth." And it came to be so.*

*And the Earth brought forth grass, the plant that yields seed according to its kind and the tree that yields fruit, whose seed is in itself according to its kind.*

––––––––––

The Earth basked in the still receding light, now coalescing and forming a bright sphere in the distance.

––––––––––

Metatron, the scribe, had called the meeting. Lucifer, the Generals and the Archangels gathered as requested, wondering what new bits of information might be presented here concerning tomorrow's parade.

Metatron began, "You have all done good work thus far; however this meeting has nothing to do with tomorrow's parade. I have been instructed to impart something to each of you. Your troops will be given these gifts tomorrow. Lucifer, please step forward, and receive your gifts."

Lucifer moved to a position directly in front of the scribe. Metatron reached out and placed his hand on the dragon's muscular shoulder. Lucifer's head curled down slowly, his neck arched up, then tilted to one side, he felt dizzy while something along his back churned under his tough hide. His spine arched upward violently, his face contorted. Teeth bared, the muscles on either side of his spine began to ripple and change, new muscles formed while new bone structure formed as well. Then six bulges began to emerge from the undulating flesh, three skin-covered nib-like structures on each side began to protrude, the skin growing as the nibs pushed out looking very much like flesh covered horns.

The Cherubim and Seraphim watched, eyes wide. Zerachiel and Azazel whispered to each other as these new spiny objects began to thicken, and lengthen, reaching a distance equal to half the length of his tail. At the end of the boney members thick knuckles began to form and a new portion of the framework began to jut more forward, muscle thickened the first portion as the new bones took shape. Distorted wrists formed at the end on this second set of bones. Then fingers jutted out from the new wrists, forming large misshaped hands. A small thumb rested right at the knuckle. A talon, matching the ones on his hands and feet, grew forward and curved down. Then the first finger pointed slightly forward and very far, the second protruded longer and slightly back, and each succeeding finger pointed more to the rear.

The sensation was difficult to describe. The process, while uncomfortable, was not painful. Looking back and forth as the six new appendages continued to grow, Lucifer's eyes widened, wondering what was happening. His teeth remained clenched as his new muscles continued flexing and relaxing with each contraction of growth.

Each finger grew very long, and a thin yet tough membrane of skin, the same red color as the rest of his leathery hide connected the fingers to each other and down from the last finger to Lucifer's back, each finger ending with a large curved talon. The contractions had ceased, and Lucifer folded them to his side and opened them fully several times, exercising the same dexterity as one would have in using hands. A wide grin covered his face.

He turned to Metatron, "What are these?"

"Wings! They allow you to fly! Flying can be much faster than walking. You will enjoy them. You were given understanding of how to use them as the wings were forming. You only need to go experiment. The next time the angel corps see any of you, you will be making a presentation at the parade. Elohim wants you to show the angel corps what these wings can do. So tonight go and experiment, then tomorrow you can put on a good show."

Metatron said with a knowing smile, "Now, I want you all to see the cherubim wings. Remiel, would you please come forward."

Still flexing his wings, Lucifer joined the other Seraphim. The generals beside him closely examined these new limbs, several reaching out to touch them.

As Remiel approached, Metatron looked toward the other angels, "Cherubim wings are unlike seraphim wings."

Metatron reached out to touch Remiel's shoulder. The Archangel felt a tingling behind his shoulders as the scribe touched him. Between the straps holding his breastplate, the angel's muscles began moving and two rather large bulges appeared. Again the nibs began pushing out, angling off more to the sides though slightly rearward. Each pushed upward several feet higher than Remiel's head, then knuckles formed and secondary bones pushed downward to another knuckle, this one much smaller than the first. Unlike the dragon wing, only a single bone exited this joint, the skin kept pace with the bones and muscles thickened the overall structure while connecting it to the angel's back. Little white dots began to appear over the surface of the new skin. Each dot or follicle pushed out white, soft, tightly-wound structures that uncoiled and stiffened, revealing almost flat plumage. This feathery covering took several minutes to grow out completely and each area of the wings receiving specific feathers, from the smaller down outcroppings closer to the skin, to very long and rigid quills near the tips. Remiel moved the wings all around, even curling the ends in front of himself.

None of the angels understood the purpose of these new wings. They had never seen anything like them in creation. None understood the concept of flight, as none had seen anything fly.

One after the other each one came forward to receive the new wings. Seraphim and Cherubim alike, though the two types of angels wings looked very different, the function was similar.

Metatron turned to Lucifer, "Commander, you need to get together with your leaders and plan for your flight demonstration. I have a few suggestions for you."

"I look forward to hearing them," Lucifer replied as he moved with Metatron to a private corner of the room.

---

He moved alone, at a brisk pace, toward the place of his birth, to spend time with the one who had made him.

Uriel ran to catch his friend and fellow archangel, "Michael! Where are you going?"

"I am going to the throne room, I need time with the Creator." Michael answered.

"Mind if I join you?"

"No, not at all, come on."

---

They stood at the back of the throne room, heads lifted, gazing at the large pillar of fire and smoke, the manifestation the Creator had chosen in this place. As they gazed, wisdom flooded into them, strengthening and teaching their hearts and minds. The Creator always gave them what they needed. He communicated to them directly to their very essence, without words, his love for them and his presence in their lives. They enjoyed these times in the throne room, and each came here often.

---

*And Elohim saw that it was good.*

*And there came to be evening and there came to be morning, the third day.*

## Chapter 13

# Day Four

*And Elohim said, "Let lights come to be in the expanse of the heavens to separate the day from the night and let them be for signs and appointed times and for days and years, and let them be for lights in the expanse of the heavens to give light on the Earth." And it came to be so.*

---

Parade day. Metatron and his aide walked through the field to mark sections with vividly colored banners, each attached to a tall pole. Elohim's scribe wanted to ensure nothing would go wrong today, especially at the outset.

"How this ceremony begins will help to dictate the course it follows," he told his aide. "By ensuring the parade starts well, we lessen the need for the troops to improvise. Do you know what I mean?"

"Not really, no, sir."

Metatron thought for a moment before attempting to clarify. "This is the first 'test' of their ability to concentrate and maintain order. Elohim Himself is providing all the distractions necessary. They will be nervous because He will be in attendance and watching. Therefore, we are trying to ensure other distractions are minimized."

"He is always in attendance and watching, is He not?" the attendant asked.

"Yes, He is, He's everywhere!" Metatron said. "However, the angelic troops will be able to see a manifestation of Him. That is what would distract them."

"I think I understand." The attendant thrust one of the banner poles into the ground.

---

The various troops began to emerge onto the parade field as the last markers were set in place. They filled the field. The contrast from two days earlier was striking. From disorder had emerged a new order, not perfect yet, but enough for this first task.

Several hours passed as the field became overwhelmed with cherubim and seraphim. The groups assumed their proper positions; each member moved into the designated place.

"Where are the leaders?" Malkiel asked.

"I do not know. I have not seen them," Jeremiel answered, beginning to wonder. "In fact, not since yesterday."

Across the massive field similar conversations spontaneously began. The whole assembly was perplexed by the absence of the Seraphim leaders and the Archangels.

Metatron, in an effort to quiet the troops, walked to the podium and called out the command... "Hosts of heaven! Attennnn-chun!"

Every single angel of the hundreds of millions present snapped to attention. The sound was thunderous.

"At ease!"

Each angel widened his stance and folded his hands together behind his back in the more comfortable position. They continued to await the arrival of the King.

Just then, one bright light appeared on the horizon directly ahead where every eye of the angelic choirs could easily see. Growing larger as it approached, a deep growl grew within. It streaked through the sky completely ablaze, wings out to the sides engulfed in blue flame: the Archangel Uriel!

He began to gain altitude, climbing thousands of feet into the air directly above the gathering, paused, then turned, and with his mighty wings launched himself directly toward the ground, pulling the fiery plumage to his sides when they had done all they could to propel him forward. His fire burned brighter than ever. He gained momentum much faster than would be possible from the effects of gravity alone. At five hundred feet from the ground he began to pull up, wings extended, slowing him enough to allow his body to pivot, landing gracefully in proper position at the front of his choir. The troops could no longer contain themselves and cheered the Archangel's display. Uriel tucked his wings to his back and stood motionless.

The dragon generals appeared next. They swooped and dove, breathing flames into the sky, spreading apart in a circle that spanned the parade field. All at once, each turned and shot straight for the center of the circle, each on a collision course with the others. As they reached the center, all of the generals in unison breathed massive fireballs toward the center of the group. Flying into the fiery explosion, they all turned abruptly in a maneuver hidden in the flames and shot straight up, then arching backwards, flying back away from the center.

The angelic choirs gasped, became silent, then cheered, enthralled with the amazing exhibition they had witnessed.

The generals broke formation and flew to their respective groups. Landing in perfect sequence, each of them gave his own signature blast of fire or shook the ground with a massive blow from his tail. All the troops cheered and talked amongst themselves about what could be expected next.

The seven Archangels flew in formation with Michael at the point of the inverted "V" pattern. Their feathery wings were different from the others seen so far. The Archangels proceeded with a range of aerial maneuvers, never breaking the pattern through barrel rolls and loops, executing each maneuver with complete precision. As Michael proceeded with a slow roll, the pattern turned as though it was attached to him. This group displayed the true meaning of order and precision. As they settled to the ground, the field was abuzz with cherubim and seraphim pointing and asking about these new limbs their leaders used.

A drone in the distance. The sound, never heard before, grew, and a lone figure in the distance flew unhurriedly toward the parade field. The large six-winged dragon moved slowly toward them. The rhythmic sound proceeded from his massive wings alternately beating the air. As he reached the head of the parade formations, he held steady, motionless. Using his wings in a way the others could not provided continuous lift while holding him perfectly still. He was in complete control and able to move in any direction he desired.

Then all at once, using all six wings in unison, he moved from stillness to forward motion. His speed increased to a blur, his body undulating with his wings' movements. He moved over the entire array of angels, above their heads. The wind from his movements causing them to re-steady themselves. He was awe-inspiring to behold, and he enjoyed showing off, enjoyed his uniqueness. Having reached the rear of the gathering, he banked to the left and headed toward the front, to his position, this time along the side opposite the stage full of dignitaries. He breathed a continuous line of fire along the ground giving the angelic formation a backdrop of flames.

As he approached his position, he once again transitioned to hovering flight and settled gracefully in position.

Cheers from the throng of angels filled the area. The sounds were melodious, and after a short time, the cheers turned into a chorus praising the Creator for what he had done.

———————

Massive gas and dust clouds throughout the new universe stirred with activity, dense regions acted like immense sink holes, growing more and more dense until pressures at the center worked to condense hydrogen, the most plentiful gas in the universe, forming helium. This fusion reaction gave off enormous quantities of energy in the form of light and heat along with other forms of radiation. These stars, as they came to be known, began bursting to life by the trillions, each fiery body swallowing up surrounding dust and gases, effectively cleaning the areas around them. The vast majority of these new stars came into being with a companion star, a smaller star linked to it by gravitational force, these "binary" stars rotated around each other and moved together through the dark universe, each couple with its own unique dance.

———————

In the darkness of Earth's night sky, small lights began to appear. A few at first, then more and more, thousands upon thousands appearing in the sky above this small planet. Most flickered and grew in intensity.

———————

The vast array of hundreds of millions of angels presented an amazing scene, all very still, patiently awaiting the arrival of the Creator. No one knew how He might present himself on this day, and all were nervous, in a good way. Of all the troops on the field, only Lucifer, his generals and the Archangels, had ever actually seen Him since the day they were made.

Above all the troops a white haze began to form, a small swirling vapor that slowly thickened and condensed onto the platform full of dignitaries until it looked like a vertical cloud stretching several miles into the sky. A bodily form seemed to almost appear, then recede back to the cloud shape. Ever in motion, this cloud was a boiling mass. A fire burst into view and the flames traveled straight up the center of the column.

One of the angels realized that this cloud seemed to be made of fire and water, just as all the angels were.

———————

*And Elohim made two great lights: the greater light to rule the day and the lesser light to rule the night and the stars.*

*And Elohim set them in the expanse of the heavens to give light on the Earth and to rule over the day and over the night and to separate the light from the darkness. And Elohim saw that it was good.*

---

"Angelic hosts of heaven!" Lucifer shouted, "Forward... March!"

The parade began, Any remaining nervousness subsided as they marched in unison. Each angel concentrated on his position, spacing, and maintenance of order. The generals and Archangels had worked out various salutes as the Creator's presence passed by the array of marching troops, and each grouping would give its distinctive salute.

The presence of Elohim lifted from the stage and spread out as it moved to the front of the marching angels. As it approached the seraphim at the front of the procession, the dragons blew great fireballs into the air and shouted, "In the service of the King!"

Michael's group held their swords high and exclaimed the meaning of his name, "Who is like Elohim!" Swords ablaze were held overhead and pointed straight up, millions of fires shot into the sky, and looked very much like millions of tiny reproductions of the central core of the Creator's presence.

---

A great fire in the sky was surrounded by nebulous clouds. Only this time the clouds were sinking into the fires and added to the mass of the newly-formed Sun. The light and heat from this, a second-generation star, Earth's closest star, would provide all the energy needed for all life on Earth throughout the ages of man.

A second sphere, closer to Earth would serve as a reflection of the greater fire in the sky, a smaller orb clothed in the light of the star, brilliant not on its own but because of the light it received and freely gave away. Serving as a calendar, it marked the months and seasons to come for all of time.

---

The cloud passed over Remiel's group last. As it did so, the troops slapped their shields with their swords, causing a ripping of thunder that swept over the group, crackling and booming.

The troops came to a halt at Lucifer's command. The parade was finished.

Metatron moved to the podium to speak, "What a fine effort all of you have demonstrated to make this parade a success."

Elohim's presence spread out and moved to cover the entire array of angels.

Metatron continued, "You have been diligent, and we appreciate all you have done over the past few days. You will now receive gifts that will propel you into the next phase of your being." Metatron paused and stepped to the side.

With that, every angel began feeling the same tingling along his back that Lucifer and the other leaders had felt. And over the course of the next several minutes, every angel became endowed with magnificent wings, each according to his kind. A growing murmur filled the assembly with the rushing excitement each angel felt at this development. Each could look and see his neighbors wings growing, some reaching out to touch them as they grew, all of them excited with this new development.

Metatron stepped back to the podium. "Now let us quiet down. I know you are all excited with how this is evolving. You will find your next phase of training to be much more exciting and probably much more painful than your former training. You need to remember you are in training, and while it will be pleasant at times, it is also important that you not skip the basics. Enough said. Let the training begin!"

"Attennn...Chun!" Lucifer shouted.

There was a short pause for the podium to clear, the cloud above them to fade from view.

"You have all done excellent work!" Lucifer paced back and forth as he spoke. "You are now ready to move on in your training. Make no mistake about it, this will be tougher, and the demands will be higher. I will give you all a period of rest, so use it wisely."

He moved to the front of his group and in a loud voice shouted, "Angelic host, Dissssss...missed!"

A roar of excitement filled Paradise.

---

*And there came to be evening and there came to be morning, the fourth day.*

## Chapter 14

# Day Five

*And Elohim said, "Let the waters teem with shoals of living creatures and let birds fly above the Earth on the face of the expanse of the heavens."*

---

Hundreds of millions of tiny animals swam in the waters of the vast ocean. Looking like reddish clouds, these gatherings of tiny crustaceans stretched for miles in all directions. Fleshy clear organisms with long dangling tentacles pulsed and undulated through the waters, in huge numbers.

Over the land great flocks of winged creatures flew. Thousands of flocks, thousands of birds in each flock, each flock was filled with birds different from those in other flocks. Swarms of smaller flying creatures buzzed about, from tiny black dots with wings to larger fuzzy multi-winged hovering insects.

In the brackish lakes boney creatures began swimming for the first time. Covered in scales or flesh these creatures began inhabiting every aquatic layer.

The Earth truly teemed with life, not just life but a staggering variety. Surely no mind but the Creator's could imagine such diversity.

―――――――

Lucifer began training his choir in the art of flight, giving each angel ample time to practice. One thing they all learned was that when the wings appeared, Elohim had also given them the knowledge to use them. All they had to do was to develop skill, which came with practice.

Once they reached a certain level of competency all the generals and archangels began teaching formation-flying. This would teach greater control as well as bring each angel's confidence level higher.

During a break several angels from Uriel's choir relaxed in a clearing.

Hillel flexed his wings, moving them all around. He lifted from the ground and spun in circles. His smile was contagious and his companions laughed at his stunts. "This is amazing! Come on! Let us see who can reach that tree on top of that hill first!"

Kallil glanced up the hill to the tree, barely within view. "We accept the challenge!"

"To the tree of life!" Said Malkiel as he lunged toward the target fifty miles or so in the distance.

With that, all three were off like three flaming darts, laughing as they flew. Each flew as fast as he could. At least that is what they thought. Malkiel looked back to assess his lead when he saw not two but three angels coming behind him, one a bit farther back but closing the distance quickly.

"Who is that?" he shouted to his two friends.

Both turned and looked behind them, Hillel yelled back, "I do not know! But he will not win!"

Moments passed. The blazing angels sent shock waves into the surface of a large lake as they flew but a few feet above its surface, the water sprayed into the air as though each of them were pulling along a fountain.

They strained ahead, the tree of life now in sight. Next to them they saw the larger blue-flamed angel pass them slowly. They each took to the challenge this stranger presented, their new-found determination causing their flames to burn hotter.

As the streaks flew overhead, other angels saw what appeared to be four blue streaks leaving long fiery trails behind them.

Kalil pushed himself beyond any limit he might have imagined for himself. His vision began to shift, objects in his view stretched and distorted as though he were bending the very fabric of awareness.

Ozel, reached the tree first, just barely. All four laughed as they slowed, making wide arcs and landing one by one next to the Tree of Life on the hill top.

"Ozel! That was amazing, you are so fast!" Hillel called out as he caught his breath.

"All of you caught on quickly and kept up with me, I did not think that would happen!" Ozel propped himself firmly against the tree with one arm, his other arm on his knee, looked at the ground, and gasped for air.

Kalil struggled to catch his breath, "When we were flying, there at the end, my vision changed."

"Yes, yes," Malkiel agreed. "I think I saw that too, was it as if everything contracted, things farther away seemed to move closer, as if the distances suddenly became shorter?"

Ozel stood up and took in a deep breath,

"I saw that too."

He looked at the others and his eyes grew wide as he realized what he was seeing, "Did you notice, all of your flames are blue now?"

---

*And Elohim created great sea creatures and every living creature that moves, with which the waters teemed, according to their kind and every winged bird according to its kind. And Elohim saw that it was good.*

---

Blue mountains rose in a rolling motion above the surface of the ocean, spouting air and water high into the sky. Massive creatures, fully one hundred feet long, were the largest animals that would ever roam the planet. Elohim had created these and their many cousins, awe-inspiring creatures matched only by their astonishing tranquility and peaceful nature.

By far the strangest creatures were made to live in the waters.

Closer to the shore, reptiles with extremely long necks swam in fluid movements and began to populate the oceans. These terrifying creatures, greatly resembling undersea versions of the dragons of heaven, were visible patrolling beside large soft boney fish, awesome in their fluidity.

In the depths of the waters there existed creatures with no bones at all, except for a small beak and hooks on its limbs, motionless, their large non-blinking eyes watching. Many of these creatures were hidden in the depths where pressure and darkness would hide them from the view of many for thousands of years to come. Waiting like presents, their very appearance would spur the creation of awe-inspiring stories, and of research that would change the world. These solitary creatures waited to be found at just the right time.

Large birds with massive wings soared high in the sky along with their reptile counterparts. Both feather-winged and flesh-winged creatures took to the air and filled the skies with life.

-----

*And Elohim blessed them, saying, "Bear fruit and increase and fill the waters in the seas and let the birds increase in the Earth."*

-----

The Cherubim groups practiced formation-flying, much as during the parade practice of former days, these angels learning the control that would be needed in the coming season.

"Sorry!" Raziel said as he collided with Jeremiel. "I must master these turns! I keep drifting..." he said, frustrated.

Jeremiel tried to reassure him, "Try banking slightly more in the turns...You are somewhat larger than most of us, you may merely need more effort to get your mass turned."

"Yes, maybe," Raziel said with his arms before him, swooping his hands through the air in an effort to visualize what his body needed to do.

———————

*And there came to be evening and there came to be morning, the fifth day.*

## Chapter 15

# Day Six

*And Elohim said, "Let the Earth bring forth the living creature according to its kind: livestock and creeping creatures and beasts of the Earth, according to its kind." And it came to be so.*

*And Elohim made the beast of the Earth according to its kind, livestock according to its kind and all that creep on the Earth according to its kind. And Elohim saw that it was good.*

*And Elohim said, "Let Us make man in our image, according to our likeness and let them rule over the fish of the sea and over the birds of the heavens and over the livestock and over all the Earth and over all the creeping creatures that creep on the Earth."*

---

Grazing animals of all kinds appeared, roaming in vast herds, as well as groupings of monstrous creatures whose long necks towered to the heights of the trees, their necks balanced by their massive tails. Packs, prides, and small groupings of animals, all the way down to the smallest walking and crawling things were created. The stage was set for the making of the creature from whom the Creator's Counterpart would come.

———————

In those days, the highest mountain was built from the rising of the earth's crust out from the oceans. As the heavy mineral laden areas sank they pushed the water beneath them to the sides. The pressure of the displaced water in turn pushed the lighter areas of ground up to reveal the uppermost portions as dry ground. The highest of these lighter areas became the mountains.

The highest mountain, was more like an enormous hill or mound. The slope was much less steep than the mountains that would rise later and it reached a height of just over 9,000 feet above the surface of the ocean waters. At the top of this great hill a depression formed that looked like a large meandering trench which surrounded the summit and cut deeply into the ground. Storm clouds often surrounded this mountain top. Lightning was visible and thunder heard for many miles in all directions.

The trench served as the watershed divide for the four great rivers of the day, the Pishon, the Gihon, the Hiddekel, and the Old Euphrates. The trench framed the central hilltop and it was here that the angels gathered.

———————

For the angels, finding the location on Earth was not difficult. Elohim was there, visible as the same pillar that had appeared on the parade platform. The pillar towered so distinctively that it was visible for hundreds of miles in all directions.

The Archangels Michael, Gabriel, and Raphael had just returned from their task of gathering a certain dry red soil found around the base of the great mound. They each placed their loads onto the ground in a heap and brushed themselves off before finding places at the front of the gathered host to observe this special event.

The air buzzed with tension, the host of heaven waited to see what Elohim would do next. Hundreds of millions of angels surrounded the location like some enormous sporting event, but this they knew was the beginning of something so important, so essential to Elohim, that absolutely everything had to be right.

Absolutely everything was right. As Elohim began to move, a hush fell over the angelic throng.

———————

The hand of the Creator moved, a portion of the huge cloud moved and swirled, pouring water upon the dry red dirt. The swirling portion grew larger and formed a whirlwind of smoke and fire which hovered just above what was now muddy clay. The wet dirt began to move and pile in areas, forming mounds of mud. The funnel cloud continued to form intricate structures within the sides of the mounds, the most minute details painstakingly fashioned. Busily working throughout the interior, the fire moved into the lumps of mud, creating structure, tissue and organs.

The process took several hours. Apparently, the Creator wanted this life form to bear His own finger prints, otherwise He would have simply spoken this new creature into existence as He did with the other earth animals.

"It looks like a small wingless cherubim," someone in the crowd ventured, while another voice said, "He's building an angel out of mud?" The murmurs quickly spread as the angels began to see what was being created.

---

When He had finished, Elohim surrounded the new being with His glory, the very clothing of the Creator Himself, and as He did so, the Creator's spirit breathed life into the mud and moved away, leaving it clothed in light, pulsating, living.

Elohim thundered across the Earth, "ARISE! Shine, for your light has come, and the glory of Elohim has risen upon you!"

Minutes passed, nothing happened. The cloud of light surrounding this new creature's body continued to churn, never still. The angels thought something had gone wrong. The new creature was not moving. It just lay there.

The Creator waited.

Angelic eyes watched, glancing toward Elohim for some sign that more had to be done, some step not finished.

The Creator waited.

The stillness became uncomfortable while all watched uneasily. As the minutes passed, many of the angels began to whisper amongst themselves. Some missed the very thing that interrupted them.

Gasping for breath, the muddy creature lifted its face from the muck. The gurgling interrupted the angels' whispers. It coughed out muddy water, fighting for air. Its back rose as it inhaled, a huge wheezing breath, and coughed several more times. Many more minutes passed while it struggled before its airways at last cleared and breathing became steady.

"What is it?" asked one of the angels. "Is it a Cherubim?"

"He has not named any of the creatures made on Earth yet," came a quiet reply.

"All of this, He has created and has not named anything at all?" the angel wondered aloud.

The second angel became more firm, continuing to watch the new creation. "No, only the creatures. He named everything else, now be quiet and watch!"

The creature moved one arm, placed its right hand on the ground next to its shoulder, elbow in the air, fingers sunk into the mud. It placed the other hand in the mud beside its left shoulder and began to rise. It was difficult to make out exactly how it moved, the undulating cloud that surrounded it hid most details, but it had an appearance that reminded the angels of Elohim himself. Somehow Elohim, whose features are so hard to see, let alone describe, had made this object with similar if not the same complexities of Elohim Himself, and He made it out of clay. It was a clay statue made in the image of Elohim, yet it had life.

---

Where there was once an empty stadium, about half way up and toward the center there appeared one single being. It remained motionless, a swirling mass of spirit, much like the swirling clouds around the Creator. It sat among the countless empty white seats staring into the towering fiery clouds.

---

And Elohim said, "It is not good for man to be alone, I am going to make a helper for him, as his counterpart".

Elohim had named something: this was the first creature on Earth to receive a name, "Man." He had also used a word unfamiliar to everyone else in creation, "Counterpart." Why did He not just make duplicates of this man, as he did with every other creature he had made?

———————

Man was given something the rest of Earth's creation did not have: a *spirit*. The very fire of Elohim moved in and around man causing him to be enveloped in wispy cloud-like light, much like Elohim's pillar of fire and smoke. Elohim spoke to man saying, "I will call you Adam, for you are the first man, and you contain all of Man. I have endowed you with knowledge and wisdom."

Taking the man east to the center of the garden in which he had made him, the Creator showed the man a certain tree. Elohim commanded the man saying, "Eat of every tree of the garden, but do not eat of the tree of the knowledge of good and evil, for in the day you eat of it, you shall certainly die.

"Tomorrow, I will rest from creation because, as for creation, it is finished. All that you see, and do not see in this earth realm was made for you."

The Angels thought they had heard wrong. "All for him? All for this one creature made of clay?"

*Didn't Elohim make all this for himself?* Lucifer thought to himself.

The entire angelic host was confused. This did not make sense. This man was not even made out of fire and water, he was dirt and water. How could all of the earth, the billions of universes, each with billions of stars, and all the creatures here on Earth, be made for this *man*? It did not seem possible, but Elohim had said it.

Elohim continued, "You will not see Me tomorrow, and I want you to enjoy this garden I have made for you. You will see Me again on the following day."

With that the cloud of the presence of Elohim dissipated.

The man was left standing, surrounded by millions of angels, most of whom were bewildered and did not understand what all the commotion was about. They slowly began leaving the assembly, heading back to the familiarity of Paradise.

One angel however stayed behind, watching this new creature. Studying him.

———————

The man became aware that he was experiencing several realities at the same time. He could sense the Creator close by, as though he were still facing him. As though while standing here, in this incredible place, with the trees and vines, grass and blue sky, he was also seated, in a magnificent and yet very different place, somehow taking in, bit by bit, the very heart of his Creator.

He became aware of three of the ways he could perceive. He could see the world around him, using his physical eyes, while also seeing another way. What he saw physically seemed to also have a different reality associated with it. Permeating everything was this higher reality, the colors were alive, everything had movement. As though everything this living One created had life in it.

Looking down at his own covering of light, he could feel a substance against his skin, he truly wore it as a garment. He realized this was different from his Creator, as the light of the Creator was a part of Him and proceeded from Him. Adam's light was in fact a garment, woven by Elohim.

Adam looked back toward the majestic red creature studying him, he could see that it existed in a way that his physical eyes could not detect, though he was plainly there, and the creature interacted with the physical surroundings. After all, it was leaning against a tree.

———————

Lucifer tried to understand what it was he had witnessed. Elohim made all of creation for this Man, the last of all created things. Aside from the swirling white mist around it, the man did not look special in any way. It was, after all, just another created beast like all the others Elohim had made in this place. Made just like them, out of clay, how could that be special?

## Chapter 16

# The Gathering

Michael and Jessica began their journey along the path directly behind her parents' home, heading northwest. The two had walked several miles and the journey took most of the morning, their progress slowed by the terrain's rolling hills, many trees and undergrowth. They crossed several fence lines and the last several hundred yards was a steady climb. Jessica's legs were complaining and she was fighting for air, as at this altitude there was less oxygen. Michael moved slowly, obviously much more slowly than he would normally travel. He showed no signs of fatigue and this thought only caused her to shake her head and smile. *He's so patient with me.*

"You don't get tired?"

Michael's brow furrowed a bit, "Of course I do."

She stepped up onto a large fallen tree which made her almost as tall as her guide. "You don't seem tired at all...and...*I* can't seem to catch my breath!" She jumped from the tree onto the ground.

He laughed under his breath, "No, it would take much more than this. It all depends upon what you are accustomed to and how you are built."

"I suppose you're right, I'm used to typing and pushing a pen!"

"We are almost there, just over this ridge you will see the clearing."

They approached the top of the hill. As she reached where Michael waited for her, he pointed downward to a grassy opening.

Jessica looked down at the clearing. "This is beautiful. So, why did we have to walk?" She was slowly able to catch her breath. "Why not just move us here as you did when I thought I would be late for class?"

"I thought you would like the view, and the exercise. You have been working rather hard, and I thought you might like to get out and see some of the surrounding woods."

She turned to look back the way they came: Pike's Peak loomed high and proud. The tree-covered hills, many capped with what looked like grassy fields dotted with deer or elk; she couldn't tell which. She could see only a few signs of civilization, the few homes amid the trees, and the little Divide strip mall in the distance. Neither seemed out of place. The view was breathtaking.

"Thank you, this is a thoughtful surprise. What's next? Why are we going to the clearing down there?"

"Another surprise. Step up."

Michael held Jessica's hand, helping her to cross several more fallen trees on their way down the hill.

As they reached the edge of the clearing Jessica thought she saw movement in the trees. She began to feel dizzy and Michael lead her to a large weathered stump to rest.

"What is that in the trees?" She squinted her eyes, trying to see the glimmer of light. She looked to her right, where several more blurred shapes among the trees were coming into focus, though she was still unable to make them out. She looked to her left, her eyes clearing to a point where she could see blurred forms, very tall angels dressed in white. Light radiated from each one. Their wings folded behind them while they walked above the ground. She stood, moved quickly to Michael's side and held his huge arm, attempting to hide behind it.

He looked down at her and smiled, "All is well, Jessica. They are friends."

"Who are they?"

"These are the rest of the archangels assigned to earth. They have come to meet you and to talk with you for a little while."

She continued watching the three figures to her left as they moved from the trees into the clearing. Her eyes focused better now. The light from these angels looked similar to when Michael had appeared to her at the light house on Cove Point. The light moved like rivers from them, filled with color, shimmering and in constant movement, living. Her eyes continued to shift, becoming better able to cope with the light that flooded toward her. The six angels moved into the clearing and formed a rough semicircle around Michael and Jessica. She stood there, an insect among giants. Her knees began to buckle and the strength left her hands, she could no longer grasp the Archangel's overcoat. He moved to catch her, to hold her up by her shoulders. She could feel strength, his strength, flowing into her. The dizziness left and he eased her back to her seated position on the stump, his hand behind her back.

Her eyes continued to adjust and she could see one of them was very different than the rest. Covered in fire, this one stayed behind the others, arms crossed. He was like the angels that had helped to ward off the dragons outside her home.

"Who is that archangel over there? The one made of fire? Is that – Uriel?"

Michael said, "Yes it is, I see you remember him from the scroll." He motioned for Uriel to come forward.

Uriel stepped forward into the center of the group, his hands clasped behind his back, his blue fire wildly raging as though in a wind storm. He was magnificent, his powerful countenance, strength of character and a hint of anger made him seem like a most amazing predator.

With her newly-found strength she stood and approached this one whom she had only imagined. Her face grew concerned as she stepped closer to him. Something was wrong. His arms and chest were covered with thousands of burning white scars. She stood within a couple of feet from the flames, her right hand, as if with a mind of its own, tracing some of the lines of the old war injuries in the air in front of him. His face sullen, eyes vacant.

Jessica commented almost silently, "What the years have done to you..." Her head tilted slightly sideways. Her glassy eyes looked to his.

Uriel's eyes moved to meet hers, his countenance unchanged. He looked at her for several seconds, then slowly shifted his eyes away, his indifference evident.

"What's wrong? You seem upset."

Uriel sighed slowly. "Whose side are you on?"

"What do you mean? I'm on the same side you're on, don't you know that?"

"No, I do not."

"How can you not know?"

Michael moved next to her, staring at his old friend. "Uriel has had a bad time since the great war, as you can see. He bears the scars from thousands of battles. His troops are as scarred as he, some more so. He is tired. Is this not so, my old friend?" Michael's stare continued.

"Yes, I am tired. Tremendously tired. Tired of your kind, tired of Man, and your sin. Your kind has cost us dearly. I will do whatever Elohim tells me to do, I just want to hear something from you."

Her eyes pleaded with him. "What's that?"

"Tell me you will not give up, tell me the attacks of the enemy, the attacks from which we are protecting you, and the ones from which we cannot protect you, will not succeed. Tell me our efforts will not be in vain. For millennia we have protected your kind, fought the traitors, suffered for the sake of Elohim. He made all this because He wants something. I want him to have it, and I am willing to fight as long as is needed to see that He gets it. Right now He has given an assignment to you...an assignment that gets Him closer to getting His desire fulfilled..." His voice trailed off, and he thought for a moment, looking past her, then spoke quietly, "Just tell me you will not give up."

Jessica looked down. His love for the Creator pierced her soul, tears welled up inside her, and somehow she knew he needed to hear this from her. She began, "I won't..."

Uriel interrupted her, "Do not look down, look into my eyes when you say it."

She looked up to gaze into the eyes of the fiery angel. Their eyes locked onto one another. She spoke the words quietly, "I won't give up."

He turned his face away. That was it, she had said it. Some of his bitterness melted away as the words washed over him. "I know it is difficult." His posture softened. "Too many times your kind has wanted to follow Elohim, only to fall into a trap, and then we watch that person decide to stay in the trap, and all that we worked for lost." His eyes shifted to her companion. "It has happened too many times, and yes Michael, I am tired of it."

"She has a better chance than many of the others."

"I know, but her heart still wavers. The enemy still has ways of getting to her."

"She cannot help that."

"I know." Uriel bowed, then turned to walk back to the rear of the group.

She continued to look at each of the towering Archangels, taking in the differences between them. Their eyes amazed her. She had not had the time to see Michael's eyes, not in this form, and the eyes before her did not change to a more human appearance. She could see what looked like dancing flames in the colors of their unblinking eyes, beautiful and never still.

"Jessica, these friends have gathered here to speak with you. We have been given permission to answer any question you might have. We do not know everything, but we can relay what we know to you."

*How can I possibly know what to ask?*

"You do not have to know what to ask right now. We will be appearing like this again, think of this as an introduction. You may find you have a few questions; however, you will be able to anticipate the next gathering and prepare for it."

One of the angels stepped toward her, a gold cord over his right shoulder lashing a shield to his back. Another gold cord crossed the first and formed an 'X' across his chest. The mouthpiece of a musical instrument protruded over his left shoulder. The angel's face was stern and yet gentle, as he approached he bowed, "Jessica, it is a pleasure to meet you, I am Gabriel. Do not fear us, we are not here to harm you. Please, ask whatever you wish."

She stared at them. She stood among angels. Who would believe her if she were brazen enough to tell anyone? Now that her eyes had adjusted to the six beings before her, she could see more readily the differences among them. Each had a spectrum of skin tones, their wing colorations and patterns were different, and each wore different garments, and some carried different armaments. All carried swords and shields of different shapes and sizes. Only a few wore helmets, several wore long tunics, and a few like Gabriel looked more like an ancient soldier, pre-Roman, with a gleaming metal breastplate.

Yet only Gabriel carried a musical instrument. His powerful physique was readily apparent, though his muscles seemed to be different from those of strong men she had seen. She was no expert in anatomy, but the muscles around his shoulders, back, and chest had a different layout. Perhaps this had something to do with the wings, which were all much larger than she would have imagined.

Standing here among them she got a sense of the magnitude of these beings. She had glimpsed angels a couple of times before, but they were always moving, or she was dizzy, or unable to focus. Now she could see, and she could only imagine this must be like being among wild predators, each of them confident and strong, unwavering in their abilities and, fortunately for her, not hunting. She considered herself fortunate to be on the same team as these humble, skilled, warriors.

She had a question, "Why has my life changed so much? So much is different now, and I don't know exactly why. I've been asked to write a novel from the scroll, yet it just doesn't seem like that big of a deal."

Gabriel stepped forward. "Whenever Elohim asks you to do something, anything at all, and you decide to do it, it is 'a big deal.' Most of your kind would not perform this task, even if they could."

"Ok, so why did He ask me?"

"You were chosen."

"But why?"

"Because you availed yourself."

*Because I made myself available.* "Ok, why now? Why not earlier in my life?"

"You are referring to when you were in school?"

She nodded.

"When you were in school, you attended a synagogue with your parents. Your heart opened to the Creator and you availed yourself. You told Him you were willing to be used by Him. You wanted Him to change the world and use you if He could. It is apparent that He could."

"How do you mean? It's been so long since that day."

"Since that moment your life has been spent in preparation to fulfill your desire. You learned to write well, learned to interpret the language you would need, and you learned to love."

*I did want God to use me. I wanted to be like Moses writing all those books.*

"And in some respects you are like him. You are one of Moses' daughters, after all."

"I am?"

Michael interjected, "Yes, you are from his line. I helped him to write Genesis, along with other scrolls, and I am helping you. He wrote scripture; you are writing a novel. So your missions are different, yet similar."

Another voice spoke up, "At the moment your heart turned to the will of Yahweh-Elohim, at that very instant, your life changed. You have been walking toward His destiny for you since that moment." The larger angel moved forward, his countenance kind, peaceful. His dark physique, mammoth.

"Why does he need me?"

"He does not need you. He wants you. He loves you. In this regard we are alike. You want to know how much He loves you? Jessica, He includes you in his plans, He does not need to do that. Take Gabriel here. He was highly esteemed by Elohim when he was sent to foretell the birth of your Messiah. Elohim could have done that Himself, but He chose to include Gabriel. He has done similar things with all of us and many of your kind as well. He includes those He loves, and many times He will wait until someone avails them self. It is not that He needs you, it is the way He chooses to work."

She looked at this massive angel, considering what he said. "What is your name?"

"I am the Archangel, Zerachiel."

Her head nodded slowly, thinking as best she could. The angels around her stood like giant pillars. "The fight at my office... what did those dragons want?"

Jeremiel spoke now, "They want you to stop interpreting the scroll. They do not want to kill you. That would be bad for them, so they are trying to get you to stop by your own choice. They want you to agree with them, through your actions. If you choose to stop, you agree with them, simple as that."

"Why do they care? So far the scroll paints them in a pretty favorable light."

Jeremiel glanced at Michael, who nodded for him to continue, "Jessica, you know what is to come in the scroll, and there are parts of what is coming that Elohim's people have forgotten. People stopped reading those manuscripts long ago. Satan would like to ensure those things stay forgotten."

Michael spoke up, "Understand, your kind was made for something Satan thought he had. Lucifer was Elohim's highest creation, until Man. Then man was given an entire universe. That did not set well with the great dragon. In his mind he deserved to be in the place your kind was given. It set him off. You will get to all that in the scroll."

Uriel moved back to the edge of the group, "I have the next answer. You are unsure of why he hates you so-Satan that is-is that right?"

Jessica nodded.

"He does not care about you. He wants Elohim to go to Hell. That is not possible, and he knows it. So he chooses the next best alternative, in his view. He is getting Elohim's image to willfully follow him into Hell, and that is what you and all your kind represent to him. He knows he is going to end up there, and he wants as many of you to join him there as possible. Every one of you he can get into the gates of Hell is more of a victory for him, almost like getting little pieces of God into Hell. He does not think of you as 'persons.' You are merely animals here on earth. He does not care about you at all. It is all about Elohim."

## Chapter 17

# Day Seven

Lucifer continued watching the man as he moved throughout the garden. He could only imagine that the man had never experienced shadows or darkness. The intense clothing in which the Creator had robed the man caused him to be the focal point of light, although the sun, and to a greater degree the moon, cloaked this Earth with shadows and darkness. These two great light sources didn't light the Earth as did the light in heaven, where no shadow had ever existed.

Shadows were all around the Man. Maybe he could see them but, if so, only as distant manifestations, not something he experienced first-hand. As the man walked, with the very light of the Creator swirling about him, the plants and trees grew faster. As he moved away, the growth rate would again decrease. Man's light produced a "growth region" that stayed with him. Everything in creation seemed to respond to man as though he were Elohim Himself. He emanated a light so similar to the Creator's that creation reacted just as it would to Elohim, even if the effect was smaller.

As the day drew on, Lucifer became more and more upset. After all, how could Elohim allow a created thing to portray itself like this? Only the Creator Himself should enjoy this sort of reception, not this...Man.

―――――――――

They had the day free. There would be no practice on this, the seventh day, only rest. The angels could spend the day however they pleased. Some went for walks in groups, enjoying the beautiful sights and sounds of Heaven. So much to see! Every nook and corner held beautiful surprises.

A larger group of Seraphim decided to explore the heavens. Earth, so different from Paradise, had intrigued them, and they wanted to see what other offerings the Heavens held. They set out in pursuit of the doorway to the Crypsis. They knew only the general direction for the passage way and they searched for many hours.

They searched in the crags, a canyon-like region filled with sheer cliffs that cut into the ground. The group spread out. They traveled over and around the land, searching the bluffs and hills.

"Over here! Is this it?"

The group made their way to the source of the shout. It was a huge recess, a cave hidden in a cliff wall, easily overlooked until they stood directly in front of it. Then the swirling light along the edges of the opening became apparent and gave way to a black center. The light moved toward the center and away from them, sinking into the darkness. It was beautiful, yet something about it made them uneasy, perhaps the blackness that appeared so deep. Blackness swallowed the light coming to it, although its strength seemed to be somehow harnessed. Thus this doorway was the extent of its reach, it could neither grow in size nor eat beyond a certain boundary.

They stood at the entrance unsure, now that they had seen it, whether they *really* wanted to enter.

"Are we going in or not?" The dragon, smaller yet heavily built, leapt from the ground and plunged into the opening.

"Guess that answers that!" a second seraphim remarked.

All of them in rapid succession flew through the entrance and into the unknown.

———

Adam thoroughly enjoyed this lush garden in which he was placed. The animals as well enjoyed being with him. A group of giant gray beasts with huge ears and long noses had walked several miles just to see this light in the distance. When they arrived, Adam's countenance so reminded them of Elohim that they bowed in his presence. "Is this Elohim in a smaller form?" The female looked away and then back, musing and then speaking: "No this isn't Elohim."

Adam looked around. He had heard them, though he was unsure if the sound came from these massive creatures or from somewhere else.

"The Creator has clothed you in a way that drew us to you, you must be very special indeed." The big male bowed once again, the female followed, "Blessings to you."

Adam knew the voices had to be coming from these animals, and he tipped his head, saying, "Blessings to you as well."

Adam was puzzled. *I can hear the animals even though their mouths don't move. Am I hearing their thoughts?*

Many of the animals, upon seeing the light that so reminded them of Elohim, made their way to Adam, at first confused at how much this creature appeared like the Creator. And throughout the day Adam continued to hear them. Somehow in his mind their voices registered in an inaudible way. Even the trees greeted him with fruit that would ripen before his very eyes, presenting their best to him. He would take from a few of the trees and eat the perfectly ripened fruit.

————————

Pulling his sword from its sheath, the blade burst into flame as it left the hilt, holding it out in front of him, he studied it turning it this way and that.

"Do not drop that!" Came a voice behind him.

He smiled at the comment, but his eyes said something different, "Why us?"

"What?"

"Why do our swords thunder? What's the point?"

"I do not know," Tzadkiel looked at Jeremiel's sword, "why were Uriel and his troops made with burning skin? Why are the seraphim completely different than the cherubim?"

"I just want to know my purpose."

"Why?"

"I want to know that I am going to matter-that it matters that I was made," Jeremiel gestured to his friend, "that we were made. We do not have the flash of the fiery ones, nor the strength of the dragons, and that does not bother me. Our swords thunder, I only want to know that there is a reason for this. Not merely that we have swords that thunder, that we are makers of noise."

"I think I understand," Tzadkiel said, nodding his head as he pulled his sword from its sheath. He glanced up from the flames of his sword.

"Let us thunder for a while..." With that, he turned, swung in a complete circle to gain momentum, and his sword cut a fiery arch through the air. With a massive thunder clap and booming crackles, Jeremiel's sword blocked Tzadkiel's. The two sparred for several hours and thunderous sounds spread through Paradise.

---

Flying through the tunnel of liquid light and passing into the darkness that was the Crypsis had a tranquilizing effect on their minds. They could hear thunder behind them, but it seemed to fade in intensity as they continued into this strange place. They pressed forward, passing from the cave into the expansive dark realm of the Crypsis. One by one they flew into rocky obstacles; others flew into the dragons that flew in front of them, until the entire group had stopped. Surveying the inky blackness, they each labored to remain in place in the black air.

"Owww! Sorry! Who is that anyway?"

"It is I. You flew into me after I hit this wall or whatever it is. It is jagged, I think I tore my wing. I cannot see anything."

"So cold here, I cannot stop shaking, the cold stings!"

Just then in the distance a brief flame flashed. There it was again, then once more. This time the flame found a place to anchor itself. The first dragon through the tunnel had apparently avoided the obstacles and moved farther into the blackness before being stopped by some rocky outcropping and had breathed a fire to see what was around him. Very quickly the idea spread, until many fires were burning, allowing the area's features to be seen albeit dimly. The ground appeared to be far beneath them. They had collided with a few of the many tall spires of jagged rock jutting up several thousand feet in the gloom. Flying down toward the base of the mounds, dampness shone throughout as interconnected puddles of dark liquid, most likely water with some sort of minerals or oil covering the surface, producing multicolored swirling patterns. A noxious smell rose from the moisture and filled their snouts. Many of them snorted in a vain attempt to rid themselves of the nastiness. Apparently the liquid was non-flammable, or the ground would have erupted violently from the many fires the dragons set as they ventured on. In any case, as they explored, either the smell had died down, or they became somewhat accustomed to it.

Amongst the great pillars they could see their breath form a cloud-like mist as they breathed and shivered. They had never experienced cold before and now found relief next to the fires they set, at least until the fires died down. They stayed diligent and kept the fires going or started new ones as they explored. It seemed the entire place was made of rocks and boulders. These great towering blades of jagged stone must have numbered in the thousands, maybe even millions, who knew? Not the slightest thing grew here. It was completely desolate, an eery place. The dragons' shapes flickered in the fire light on the barren rock, along with the fires and mist from their breath. This was a scene never before witnessed.

––––––––––

The sun began to set. Adam sat alone on the side of a gentle slope, holding a tawny animal of some sort. He enjoyed rubbing its long ears, while its mate lay next to his legs.

"I do not know what to call you, little creature." Then it came to him, "I will call your kind Rabbit."

Adam inhaled slowly, filling his lung with the fragrant air before pushing the air out again, just as slowly.

"I wonder what wonders tomorrow will bring." He could not help marveling at the amazing world his Creator had given him. Astounding, Elohim had made all this and then handed everything to him. It was so much to absorb, and he was certain he could never see it all even if he walked forever. All that he saw, and all he had not seen yet, were his. He wondered what all this meant.

Looking around, he also could not help noticing that various angels had returned. Some stood at a distance talking quietly in groups and occasionally glancing toward him, others were alone, peeking out from behind trees or bushes. Neither of the two types of angels tried to approach him or interact with him; they all kept their distance. It was more as if they were studying him, as if he represented some interesting problem to resolve. Elohim was up to something, and Adam did not understand any more than they did.

"I suppose we shall all find out soon." He looked down and rubbed the ears of his new little friend.

## Chapter 18

# Day Eight

The sun had slipped below the horizon only moments before. The Eighth day was beginning, and the stars were out in all their glory.

Adam saw something amongst the stars in the dimming sky. A light flickered. It was larger than the other stars in the sky, and it continued to grow as he watched, until it exploded toward the earth. The fire crashed into the ground, sending shockwaves through the earth and dust flying into the air. Adam had to crouch to maintain his balance. Even as the top stretched many miles into the sky, smoke and steam flowed outward, the huge column filled Adam's view.

Adam began to smile. This was the One Who had created him, the One Whom he continued to see as some part of him sat elsewhere, the One he continued to learn about as he gazed into the flames. Adam wondered if the animals could ever treat him like this

One. He knew that the light that emanated from his garments could in no way match the spectacular array before him now.

The inner pillar of fire rapidly changed. Unlike the smoke that billowed out from the flames in a steady stream, the flames in the center appeared to be out of harmony with time. He watched as they jerked forward and backward in and out of time. Finally, he closed his eyes and basked in the glow of his Creator.

Thunder erupted from before him, "Adam, today you are going to start naming all the various kinds of creatures I have created," Elohim said with excitement in His voice.

The man looked down at his little friend, widening his eyes. The rabbit looked back at him.

"I see you have already begun. Good. Are you ready to get to work?" Elohim asked in a quiet thunder.

The man turned back to his Creator, "I am."

As soon as he said it, he was whisked away, scooped up into a whirlwind, as Elohim carried him over a far-away ocean.

"Adam, today you will name the sea creatures." They plunged into the water where all manner of life flowed into the Creator's presence. As the sea creatures passed, each bowed before their Creator and his representative, Man. Adam gave them names, each according to their kind.

So many creatures to name! Each kind passed before him in pairs. Male and female, he named the whales, sharks, sea turtles, squid, crabs, and vast schools of fish all the way down to plankton and krill. The list went on and on throughout that entire Eighth day. Male and female of each kind paraded before him, and he somehow named them all. It was as though the names were already in him, tucked away in a treasure box waiting for him to distribute.

Adam noticed something else during this day of work, something he had experienced the day before. He could sense something in these creatures. Language, almost. He could hear their intentions. All seemed to relate how blessed they felt to receive names.

---

"Show me what you have found." Lucifer quietly ordered his General.

"This way, Sir." Semyaza turned and began running, a rhythmic gallop, then leapt into the air and flew toward the cave, his Commander behind him. As they flew, several of the others that had previously made the trip saw the two flying in the direction of the Crypsis entrance. They took to the air to follow along, calling to others beneath them as they passed by. As they neared the cavity, Lucifer slowed, settled to the ground and looked intently at the large entrance, landing about thirty yards from it. The opening seemed to have a hypnotic effect on the Commander who stood and looked into the blackness for quite some time.

"And you all went in there?" Lucifer asked, his face and eyes remaining fixed upon the entrance as he spoke.

"Yes, sir."

Lucifer studied the swirling colors and the completely dark center before saying, "All right, let us go."

Semyaza escorted his commander through the entrance. The light danced around them as they continued through the long tunnel. Emerging out the other side Lucifer hovered in the darkness, the other dragons passing by him. Fires quickly began to appear, showing the layout of the expansive dark place. The dragons were eager to see their commander's impression of this dark and damp world. All together there were now several hundred dragons with them.

Lucifer did not seem to mind the crowd. He seemed distant, caught up in his own thoughts. Semyaza watched his commander, wondering what might be preoccupying him.

Hovering, the Commander moved toward one of the spires and scratched off a bit of crusty rock, eyeing it in the light of the flames. His head tilted, barely. His head followed his eyes upward. He looked toward the gnarled top that came to a point, then looked past this first tower to see that many more stood beyond it. A sea of sharp pinnacles lay before him, looming in the blackness.

His head tilted down as he continued his survey of the area. He noticed the moisture on the ground below them and descended slowly. He touched down and in one smooth motion crouched to scoop up some of the liquid into his hand. The liquid flowed back into its puddle as he slowly curled his fingers, feeling the liquid. He rubbed his hands together, then rubbed his fingers together, feeling the slickness of the fluid. He lifted his left hand to his snout, sniffing several times. He remained motionless for several seconds, except for his eyes: they looked up and to the right, then to the left.

"Why did He create this place?" Lucifer wondered quietly.

"Sir?" asked the general.

"What do you suppose is the reason Elohim created this dark world?" He asked again, addressing the question half to the General and half to himself.

"I have never thought to ask *why* He created *anything*, sir." Came the reply.

"You would do well to think about it." Lucifer said sternly, obviously irritated. The Commander's scowl was highlighted by the low lying flickering light.

## Chapter 19

# Day Nine

The Eighth day bled into the Ninth day and the underwater adventure continued. Adam's mind reeled as he watched the incredible array of life that streamed before his eyes. His Creator, beside him in the great depths of the ocean, was happy to allow this created man to assign names to what He had made. The oceans were filled with so many different kinds of life.

Once finished in the depths, Elohim moved Adam to a beautiful area of shoreline where he was able to name the coral and all the smaller creatures that inhabited this region. He named the hermit crabs who were still choosing their shell homes, the eels and shrimps, puffers, rays, and tangs, a vast array of sea creatures in such a limited space.

———

Metatron walked onto the balcony outside his chamber. The Commander, Lucifer, had arrived a few minutes earlier and stood looking out toward the parade field.

"Lucifer, your generals and archangels have done fine work getting everything in order, and I am sure all the things learned so far will solidify into greater order in the time to come. Do you not agree?"

"I do. They will all become more confident as they use the skills we have taught them."

"With that in mind, Commander, I shall assign positions to the different choirs. I want you to assemble the troops, so they can receive their assignments later this afternoon."

"Yes, sir." Lucifer's eyes remained focused on the field.

"Is something bothering you, Commander?"

Lucifer thought for a moment, *Should I ask about the Crypsis? No, it was created for a reason and I need to find that reason, on my own.* Lucifer turned to face the scribe. "No, sir, everything is good."

"Very well, you are dismissed, Commander."

Lucifer turned back toward the edge of the balcony, spread his wings, and took to the air.

———

Four hundred and forty-four messengers were sent throughout the earth to gather the angels to the meeting, and an equal number spread out through Paradise on the same mission.

The Commander waited on the parade field with several of his generals. Making contact with Azazel, he motioned for the general to walk with him. The two walked away from the rest of the group and

Lucifer leaned toward Azazel. "General, send messengers to the Crypsis, retrieve the seraphim that are there." Lucifer said, his voice quiet.

"Yes sir, I'll get them here."

———————

Two Seraphim flew north toward the parade field, where a big announcement was to be made at the meeting. Malkiel and Hillel flew just behind and below these two. The sky was full of angels making their way to the parade field. The smaller seraphim motioned to the west.

"It is in that direction, hidden in some cliffs. If you want to see it, I will show you."

"Certainly. Suppose we go after the gathering?" The larger dragon asked.

"All right. there will be others as well. Find me after the meeting, and we will all go together." He paused for a moment, "Do you know what this gathering concerns?"

The larger Seraphim shrugged. "No idea."

Malkiel glanced over to Hillel and both wondered about this mysterious place about which the Seraphim were talking.

———————

As the angels gathered, Lucifer paced back at the front of the gathering. He tried, without any success, to maintain the appearance of calm. He kept looking out to the west of the parade field, then his head would turn, and he would shake it back and forth slowly, continuing his back-and-forth vigil.

He turned his head for what must have been the twentieth time when finally, something caught his attention. His shoulders relaxed, and his anxiety dropped away.

A large group of dragons approached the field and settled into their positions. Azazel lead the group and once all the Seraphim landed, he approached Lucifer with a salute.

---

Two Generals flew toward the field. "It is rather strange, don't you think?" Semyaza, a large grey dragon said to the smaller, tan-colored. Ezeqeel.

"What is strange?"

"Elohim created so much in the earth realm, and we really have not seen much of it yet. He created all of it, then he gave it all to the last creature he created. A creature made of mud...dirt, of all things. He made this figure of himself, and then gave everything to it." He paused, looking away, "I do not know, but the idea just struck me in an odd way. I do not know what all this is for."

The tan dragon nodded, scowling slightly, then replied, "Do you expect Him to tell you all His plans? Come on, we need to get in place."

The two dropped down into their positions just before Metatron approached the assembly.

---

Metatron began, "Troops, I want to commend you for completing your tasks. You have learned more than you realize. You have learned what it takes to bring order from chaos. When we began, as a group of angels, you were chaotic. No order whatsoever, and now look at you. In a short time you have learned the meaning and the value of order, and you have learned to work together. These are valuable lessons."

He continued, "Today I will assign your choirs to different parts of creation. Your assignments have two parts: First, you will learn everything you can about the place where you are assigned. For instance, if you are assigned to the Sun, you will go and learn about that particular star, learning how it works, what are its functions and what are its many properties. You will need to confer with your fellow angels, not just those in your group. Feel free to discuss your findings with others who may have information you need. Your group will develop the most complete awareness possible. This is a time of discovery for you, you will be learning about the Creator by studying the creation. Watch and learn, that is your assignment. It is the dawning of the age of the Watchers."

Semyaza looked down and repeated the words, "The Watchers."

"Second: You will in the future be given the task of teaching the race of man concerning these things you have learned. Therefore, you will need to again bring order from chaos. You will organize your information in a clear and methodical way that will enable you to teach men.

"One last point, and I want to be perfectly clear here. You are not to teach man ANYTHING, until told to do so. I hope I am making myself clear on this point, obedience is imperative."

He paused to let the last statement soak in.

"Good," Metatron began again, "let us begin."

"Lucifer, as head of the Seraphim, you are assigned the throne and throne room. You are to guard the Glory of Elohim. You are to place guards surrounding the throne, at least four should be there at all times."

Lucifer bowed his head in recognition of his task and the high honor it meant.

"Michael, you are to guard the glory of the image of the Creator. Your assignment is on Earth, and you are to cover and protect the Creator's Man. You are to assign angels to the people of Elohim, as guardians, so nothing shall befall those who are His. You are the protector of all who are like Elohim."

Michael bowed. *There is only one man. Seems a simple task.*

"Gabriel, you are to guard the word of Elohim. You are made to be, and your function will be as messenger of Elohim to man's kind. Your assignment will carry you back and forth between Paradise and Earth. You will bear the very words of the creator, announcing His plans and purposes for those He loves."

Gabriel bowed.

"Raphael, you will carry the healing virtue of Elohim. Your assignment is to tend to the physical and mental needs of mankind. You will be moving with the very love of the Creator for His people, and in your task, it is imperative that you only move as He leads."

Raphael bowed.

"Uriel, as you may have already gathered, you will carry the fire of Elohim. You are the front line of Elohim's offense and you are the conviction that brings restoration. This will become clear in the future. Your assignment will carry you throughout creation receiving assignments and carrying them out with great haste. Speed is always important for you."

Uriel bowed.

"Raguel, you carry the essence of the friendship of Elohim. You will learn and instruct mankind in the ways of friendship but, equally important, the ways of justice, fairness, and how to live in harmony with one another."

Raguel bowed.

"Zerachiel, you have two assignments. The first is that you are to protect the children of Men. This part of your assignment will overlap with Michael's assignment; however, you will be only looking toward the children to protect them. Your second assignment will come at a later time."

Zerachiel bowed. *Children, hmmm, what are children?*

"Remiel, you carry the sound of Elohim. This is not the same as the message of Elohim. You carry the annunciation and character of His words. You will take the very sound from the throne room, when appropriate, and you will release it on the Earth. You also have a second assignment that will be revealed at a later time."

Remiel bowed.

"Troops, I want to give you three pieces of advice for your respective journeys. Please take these to heart:

"Do not allow your hearts to harden.
Remain soft and pliable
before your Creator.

'Do not close your eyes.
Always allow the light of heaven
to pass through them,
for only His light
can illuminate your inward parts.

'Do not stop listening
to the Word of the Creator
and His Spirit.
Always allow Him
to guide you
in all you do."

Metatron lifted his gaze to the sky and said, "All praise, and all power, and all authority, belong to the Creator of all." He quietly collected his notes.

Lucifer moved up the steps to the podium. Clearing his throat, he turned to face the Angelic throng. "Today we have been given our permanent assignments. It has been a pleasure leading you, and as of now, the Archangels will be the supreme commanders of their own ranks, equal to myself. As we will no longer function in the hierarchy of these past days, it is no longer necessary. Again, it has been a pleasure.

"Archangels, as my last act of leadership over you, I release you from my command."

Lucifer moved from the podium to the front of the Seraphim, "I need twelve volunteers." Thousands of hands went in the air. Lucifer looked to the front of the group and called the first twelve he saw. He quickly split the group in two, "You eight on my left, you are assigned to the four gates of the throne room. No one enters or leaves without one of you knowing. Two of you should be at each gate. That way one can detain those wishing to enter and the other can seek instruction if none has already been given." He looked at the other four, "You four are assigned to the throne itself, space yourselves about the throne."

He backed away from the main group to allow more privacy and motioned for the twelve to gather around him. "Your assignment does not end until you are replaced. Understood?"

The twelve responded together, "Yes sir!"

"Excellent. You are dismissed to your assignments."

With that, the twelve dragons lifted off from the ground and made their way to the palace, taking up their new positions.

Lucifer looked to the main group of seraphim before him, called them to attention, and dismissed them.

Michael turned to face his angels and addressed them. "Cherubim, we have been given a high honor today. Upon your dismissal here, you are to gather your things, and we will reunite at the divide, on the tenth day, midday. Understood?"

"Yes sir!" the choir shouted back to him.

"Choir!" Michael shouted, "Atten...chun!" He waited for the silence that signified the order had been carried out, then he shouted, "Dismissed!"

---

"Did that answer your question?"

"What?" Jeremiel turned his head quickly to see Tzadkiel behind him.

"Did that answer your question, you know, about your purpose?"

"Oh right, I have been thinking about it. So, we are to convey the sound of the Creator to the Earth. I am not sure what that means exactly."

Tzadkiel gripped his friend's shoulders, and looked straight into his eyes, "It looks like we have a purpose, even if it is not clear yet. My guess is, it has something to do with our swords thundering."

Jeremiel smiled.

---

Michael made his way to the other archangels, each had dismissed their choirs and were talking amongst themselves. As Michael walked closer, he began to overhear one of the conversations. Remiel was talking with Gabriel, "You think I should make an appointment with Metatron?"

"I do, you would not want to get it wrong, would you?" Gabriel responded.

"What is going on?" Michael asked.

"You heard Metatron," Remiel explained, "I am supposed to carry the voice of the Creator."

"Yes, and...?" Michael inquired.

"How exactly is that done? My choir has to carry the sound of His voice? I have no idea what that means." Remiel replied.

Michael's eyes widened, "I am with Gabriel. Go see Metatron."

---

Once the sea creatures were named, they moved on to the small inland seas and lakes, as the man continued naming the water insects, crustaceans, and lake fish. These fish again were vast in number, and again Adam continued to name these creatures. As before, the pairs lined up to bow to their king, greet the King's ambassador, and receive their names.

All at once it occurred to Adam: everything he had named so far had a mate, they were all in pairs.

He turned to the Creator of all things, "How come they are all..."

Elohim interrupted. "It is all right, Adam, stay with your work. You're beginning to understand."

The man turned back and continued to name the fish, now with a strange idea in the back of his mind.

———————

"So He has set a guard over His glory and with the same brush stroke set a guard over his little clay Man's glory." Lucifer thought out loud, not shouting, though not keeping his voice to himself either. "At least I do not have to be the one to serve this...*man*. Although I feel badly for Michael, he deserves better."

His generals could not help but overhear his words. They were all glad to be in the service of Lucifer and that Lucifer's assignment kept them next to Elohim. They certainly did not want to be serving this image of Elohim either.

"He created everything on that earth and then gave it all to the last beast created there." His emotions overwhelmed him. "And now even the angels are called to serve this dirt man! We walk on dirt! How dare He ask one of my Archangels to do this, it is beneath them!" He grew louder as he spoke, "What is next? Will He ask us to worship this graven image?"

The forest clearing was filled with Seraphim who were in complete agreement. Lucifer's outrage made sense to them. Man was beneath them yet now many of the angels were told to serve him! None of Elohim's recent actions made any sense at all.

# Chapter 20

# Whispers

Walking through the bright lights and swarming people, Jessica was filled with wonder. She loved the sights and sounds of the fair, the rides spinning, soaring and twirling, even the lines of people waiting for their chance to be tossed in the air. She watched as a little boy and his mother exited the ferris wheel. His smile was contagious as he stopped, turned and pointed toward the people still at the top of the wheel.

"We were up there, Mommy!"

She lifted him up in her arms, whispering something into his ear and pointing along with him.

Jessica continued walking, passing a pair of teenage boys chomping on roasted turkey legs; they looked like cavemen eating from a fresh kill. She laughed to herself at the idea and continued past the funnel cake stand, the deep-fried corn on the cob booth, and a couple of tee-shirt booths. The first booth had a big heated iron press for stamping pre-made vinyl lettering onto shirts. The second housed a young man airbrushing an exquisitely-rendered late sixties muscle car backdropped by a World War Two era fighter plane sitting above a slogan that wasn't finished enough to decipher. She marveled at the amount of effort going into a tee-shirt. The man seemed oblivious to all the commotion outside his little booth.

Without realizing it, and before she knew it, she was walking in the shadows outside the fair, beyond the perimeter. The sights and sounds had dimmed behind her. She began to hear whispering in the shadows. She couldn't make out what the voices were saying but felt compelled to move forward.

Finding herself in an alleyway, she walked past a trash dumpster to her left and could see the street was damp as she continued, the only light coming from street lights now behind her. The whispers grew louder though they remained unintelligible, and now they were coming from all around her. She stopped, this time seeing the shadows slither and writhe toward her along the building's brick walls and windows. She could see no bodies, only the shadows.

She stopped and began walking backward slowly, then turned to leave. The shadows continued toward her. The way she came was now inexplicably blocked by a brick wall. Looking first to one side and then the other, she couldn't find a way out. The shadows in the road began to close in around her. Turning back to face the alley she saw it at last. A monstrous dragon.

In its coiled state, the dragon was still the height of the four-story buildings which surrounded it.

Scales shimmered on the lighted side of its massive and yet gaunt body. Many individual horn-like projections formed a row single file down the center of its skull, two emerging from the same opening, though one was broken off. The creature's vast wings filled the area between itself and the buildings to either side. The eyes glowed yellow-green while grotesque phosphorescent fumes smoldered from its mouth.

The massive beast reared its head back, its chest swelling. The filling of its lungs permeated the air with an eery shrieking sound. Then, aiming its head directly toward her, it lunged, its mouth opening wide just before she saw a mammoth fireball form and fill her vision.

---

"Ahhhhhhhh!" She awoke already sitting up. Her eyes danced around the room frantically. She couldn't remember where she was. Looking down in the darkness toward her hands, she realized she was grasping her extremely soft comforter. Releasing both hands, she smoothed out the covers and took in a deep breath, her heart still pounded against the cage of her ribs. Her eyes continued to scan the room quickly in the darkness.

"That was just a dream. Just breathe, Jess," she coached herself. It took her several minutes to catch her breath, and in that span she wiped the sweat from her brow several times.

Lying back down, she closed her eyes, trying to put that last dream behind her. In the darkness she heard it again, the whispers from her dream were here in the room. She couldn't make out what they were saying and pulled the thick covers up under her chin, all the while listening.

———————

A ring of lights, roughly two hundred yards in diameter surrounded the house. One of the lights, a guardian, Karmiel, listened as the Spirit of Elohim spoke a very simple message to his heart, "My daughter needs you." His head, and all his senses, turned to the small house. He now sensed that one of the women inside had awoken and not drifted back to sleep as people normally did. He could feel her consciousness, her tension. Something, somehow must have gotten through. Calling to the two guardians closest to him with a small chirping sound, he motioned for them to move closer, covering his absence as he moved toward the house, leaving his post as part of the perimeter guard. The two complied without hesitation. His light began to dim as he faded into the darkness of this moonless night.

The hundred or so yards passed quickly. He was a master of stealth. Blending with the dim lighting and shadows was an art form, and his experience was vast. His movements were meticulous as he progressed between the aspens and fir trees, weaving his way toward the home.

Stepping up onto the small front porch he leaned close to the house, placed his large hands gently on the stucco as he turned and tilted his head to listen through the wall. There it was, a faint guttural gurgling sound he'd heard many times before. Stepping through the front door, the large heavily armored being's countenance shifted once again to match the darkness inside. As though a cloak had been thrown over him, he now blended with the shadows, his light all but quenched. Slowly, deliberately he moved through the house, without regard for walls or other structures. The rasping voice became more pronounced as he advanced. Easing through the guest bathroom, standing with the sink surrounding the lower half of one leg, his knee just above the countertop, he froze, crouched. The creature that kept her awake was now within view. His keen vision pierced the sheetrock and lumber of this structure. Lying beneath her bed, indeed inside the floor under her, a coiled and flattened beast lay hidden, choking and spitting out lies in a language unknown to her mind, but obvious to her spirit. She laid there tense, trying to listen when listening was the last thing she needed to do.

He watched as the small sickly green dragon lay beneath her continuing to spew lies into her that could take days or weeks to filter into her consciousness. These lies, always delivered in multiple layers, one layer covering the next, many layers deep, would wind an intricate self-supporting web of falsehood, skillfully tied into truth she already knew and believed.

The serpent's head was facing away from the guardian, and apparently it had no awareness of the angel's approach. The way its head bobbed up and down in rhythm with the words looked as though it had lulled itself into some kind of trance. The seraphim's present condition could be used against it, and again the angel moved, only this time he eased through the floor and down to the basement beneath the dragon and Jessica's room. He found himself crouched in the hallway outside of Belle's room. His careful progression continued for another thirty seconds until he was directly beneath the tail of the serpent.

The angel, crouched under the coiled monster, kept his head just below the ceiling of the main floor, his hand moved up toward the beast's tail. When his hand was just below the green scaled serpent, he paused just long enough to take in a slow deep breath.

The serpent stopped. He must have sensed the massive presence beneath him. His head instantly turned. Seeing the big angel, he uncoiled and shot toward the closest wall. Too late.

The angel, instantly bursting with brilliant white light, grabbed the serpent by the end of its tail. The angel's face grimaced in pain feeling the long blade like horns projected from the dragons tail piercing through his vise like grip, spewing molten liquid into the air. Realizing escape was futile the dragon whipped his body back toward its predator. His jaw opened and headed straight for the angel's throat. A huge left hand rose in an instant to block the razor sharp teeth headed for him and caught the dragon by the snout. The angel quickly dropped to the floor driving the skull of the little beast into the ground. The lower jaw broke loose from the guardian's grip, shrieks of pain filled the atmosphere. The dragon's jaw chomped wildly trying to gain any sort of advantage, the snapping sounds permeated the air like a hundred bear traps simultaneously springing closed over and over. The angel pushed harder on the upper jaw, his wings braced against the ceiling for added leverage, crushing the snout into the skull. The dragon lay still leaving the angel to pry the horns, of the now limp tail, from his right hand. The tail flopped to the floor of the basement, then the entire body sizzled and crackled as it transformed into a dissipating pale yellow stench.

---

The whispering stopped. She tried harder to hear whatever it was, but it was gone. She could only imagine that it was a leftover remnant from her dream, *I must have imagined it*. She lay in silence for several minutes until a calmness overtook her. Her eyes again felt heavy, and the panic from her nightmare seemed to slip away.

---

The angel climbed through the floor to her bedroom, his wounded right hand bound with some sort of cloth. He stood in the corner closest to the foot of her bed and slowly moved his brown and tan striped wings back and forth, fanning her. The spiritual breeze soothed her mind and cleansed the evil that was placed deep within.

---

She woke around seven o'clock, the smell of something cooking helped her to her feet. She picked up her robe from the end of the bed and put it on as she slowly walked out of her room and down the hallway toward the kitchen.

"Belle?"

"Good morning sleepy head! You slept in today! I knew you were up last night so I decided to make you breakfast."

Jessica walked from the hallway, through the entry way and into the dining room. The table was already set. Belle came from the kitchen with two plates, setting both at the table.

"Have a seat, your coffee is on its way, I'll be right back."

Jessica sat at the head of the table. The position to her left was set as well.

"Thank you, Belle. This is completely unexpected."

"No problem at all." Belle emerged once again with two delicate glass cups of coffee, placing one in front of Jessica. "I made it just like you like it."

Belle took her place at the table, bowed her head and said, "Thanks God, we love it here, bless the food, please. Amen."

Belle picked up her fork and was just about to cut into her perfectly cooked eggs when she noticed Jessica wasn't moving.

"What's wrong?"

"Was that a prayer?"

"Uhhh, yeah. Eat!"

"Sorry for my confusion, I guess I'm not used to prayers being so informal I guess."

"Well, it's like my Dad used to say, 'Pray what'cha mean, nothin' more,' so I keep it simple and straightforward."

"Sounds good to me. So what have we here?"

"I made eggs, over easy, cooked with olive oil, the greens are baby spinach leaves sauteed in olive oil as well with a little salt, and of course tomato slices. I just wanted to make you a good breakfast since I know you didn't sleep well."

"You're very thoughtful. How did you know?"

"How did I know what?"

"How did you know I woke up in the middle of the night?"

"Well, I woke up too, I heard some sort of low airy voice kinda sounds, creepy, then after several minutes you came downstairs and turned on the light in the den. I saw it under my door. Then after some bumping around, it was quiet again."

"Belle, I didn't go downstairs. I stayed in my bed. I heard the same sound though. I thought it sounded like whispering. Then it was suddenly gone."

"Right, it stopped right before the lights went out. I didn't even hear you go back up the stairs."

"Belle, I didn't leave my bed."

"Then who turned the light on?"

"I don't know."

## Chapter 21

# Day Ten

They sat together on a small hill facing a large lake. The man had just finished naming all the creatures living in the water.

"Adam, what do you think so far?" the Creator asked.

"I am overwhelmed," he stated flatly, looking at the water. "How did you come up with so many creatures?"

The Creator didn't respond, and the two sat quietly for what had to be several hours. Then the Creator said, "Are you ready to name the creatures of the air?"

The man glanced into the sky, then he turned to the One who had befriended him and said, "Lead the way!"

---

Hillel glanced around, looking for something. Not finding whatever it was, he flew, leaving a fiery streak in the sky, over the various practice fields, each field either vacant or blessed with various cherubim practicing the intricacies of flight. He continued on, scanning as he flew.

Finding his friends, he began his descent, and came to rest several yards from them, on a hill that overlooked a great sea, smooth as glass. Everything in this place seemed to rest. Walking over to them, he called out "Hellooooo!"

"Hello there!" Kalil yelled back.

Ozel walked toward him, "Where have you been?"

Hillel was excited and his words came faster than he would have liked. "I started out this morning thinking about the Seraphim-"

Kalil interrupted, scowling a bit. "What about them?"

"Have you seen any of them?"

"Yes, they were at the field yesterday." Kalil responded.

"Yes, but do you see any now? I mean *any*?" Hillel asked.

Ozel motioned toward the throne room. "There are the eight at the entrances to the throne room, four surrounding the throne."

"Yes, but I found out from one of the gate guards that they have been there since the announcement. They have not had a normal rotation." Hillel seemed to become more agitated as the moments passed. "I mean, it is as if their leaders had vanished or forgotten them. Not that they mind, it is a good assignment." Hillel continued to look around.

"How do you hide a hundred and thirty million dragons?" Ozel asked, turning to look westward, in the same direction as Hillel.

———

Michael arrived fresh from Earth, eager to meet with the scribe and give his report. Metatron entered the room and asked him how matters were going.

"We are organized and ready. Once the man and Elohim have finished, we will be in place, set to start."

"Good, good, I am glad to hear it. How are your angels liking Earth?"

"It is beautiful, different in some respects from this place but still incredible. They like it." Michael smiled as he thought of their new home.

"I brought you here because there's something I need to tell you."

This statement caught Michael's attention, his eyes sharpened.

"Michael, you are a faithful Archangel and your mission will grow in ways you cannot image right now." Metatron shifted slightly, his eyes became sad as he stared off into the distance. "You must remember, Elohim will never give you more than He already has given you the strength to handle. He has already prepared you for everything you will ever face. Remember that, will you?"

"Yes sir, but can you tell me to what you are referring?" Michael stepped forward.

"I am sorry, I cannot. I can say this though, everyone reaches a point where they must make a choice, they may get only one, but they do have at least one choice. The Creator will not decide for them, and their choices directly determine their future." He paused for a moment. "Things have already begun that cannot be reversed. Choices have already been made, and these choices will affect you, your choice is coming."

"Will I know when my choice comes?"

"You may not in the moment realize the significance of your choice, although in the moment is not when the choice is truly made." He paused to let the words sink in, "The choice is made before the event by your actions and habits. Your behavior leads you into your future." Metatron turned to leave, pausing to say, "Michael, you have nothing to be concerned about."

Michael watched the scribe leave the room, then he looked out, in silence sorting through his words.

———————

After Michael left the meeting he had no better understanding than when Metatron had departed. He walked in the direction of the Throne Room. He wanted to be in the glory of Elohim again before returning to Earth.

He walked along the heavenly street, his golden reflection under his feet. He gazed toward the building he would soon enter. The entire structure was a living thing, or many living things, who could tell? It seemed to breathe. The great columns soared into the sky, as if they were alive, as if the earthly Sequoias had moved to form this great hall, standing at attention, basking in the glow of the Creator that dwelt inside. He climbed the jewel-like stairs leading to the towering entrance, and one of the guards held a door open for him. A door within a door really, as the main doors, made from a single pearl, could allow for thousands to pass through quickly, whereas this was a single door an individual could pass through. As he approached the two Seraphim guards at the entrance to the throne room, both saluted him crisply.

Michael returned their salute, "Greetings!"

"The Lord bless you," they said as he passed, and the seraphim who held the door closed it gently behind the archangel. The two settled back to their post.

Michael rose into the air, then just as quickly dropped back to the floor, having covered only a short distance. *I think I will walk.*

———————

The atmospheric changes were continually refreshing as he walked. Approaching the focal point of the room, he saw the sea between himself and the throne. Behind him, along the living walls, great balconies on both sides of the massive doors spanned the rear of the room. This throne room was only slightly smaller than the main parade field and was able to accommodate every angel with plenty of room left over. Nearing the large body of water, his birth place, he could sense Elohim's spirit moving through him more and more. If he would have flown, he might have missed some of the subtleties of these moments.

———————

A smaller dragon flew through the recess in the cliff, through the blackening tunnel and into the completely black Crypsis, his occasional flame bursts the only thing allowing him to avoid collisions with the jutting rocks and cave walls. Exiting the tunnel, he saw many lights in the distance. One of them was larger than the others, and he flew toward it.

He was right, the light was a larger fire, or rather many large fires, and a large group of dragons were gathered there. He paused for a moment to look at the group. He was searching for someone in particular and, spotting his target, he flew around the outside of the group and landed just behind the commander, Lucifer, to whisper something important in his ear.

Lucifer turned slowly and said, "Where is he?"

"He is in the throne room now."

"Tell me when he returns to Earth." Lucifer commanded as he turned back to the others.

The small dragon bowed as he slowly backed away. With a powerful surge from his wings he headed back toward Paradise.

---

Michael continued the long walk to the throne. Wave after wave of peace and joy kept flowing through him. His head was bowed as he came to the edge of the water. He moved toward the bridge just to his left and began to cross over. The bridge arched high into the air, and the water below had the appearance of aquamarine. Reaching the top of the bridge, he saw seven massive oil-filled lamps, each burning with a slightly different color, and the fragrances were amazing and sweet. One scent he had smelled before, on Earth. He was sure it was the scent of the peach tree!

The four Seraphim angels were surrounding the throne, but something about them had changed: they were no longer facing away from the throne, they had all turned and were staring directly at the throne, each of them murmuring something. Their wings were outstretched very wide and curved toward each other. Surely these were the most massive of the seraphim. Their bodies glowed and their gaze was so intense that the light of Elohim Himself seemed to be flowing into them. He tried to understand what they were muttering but could not.

Above the seraphim was a ring of charged green swirling gas, as though emerald powder were trapped in the air as it whirled violently. From this spinning green cloud came incredible bolts of lightning, crashing all around the throne with crackling thunder exploding from the light. Around the throne were 24 smaller thrones, all empty and looking small enough for man to occupy. Surrounding all this was what appeared to be a great stadium, filled with seats, man-sized. He wondered what the empty seats were for; who would sit in them. Then he saw one seat filled. A spirit sat in the stadium seats, alone, staring into the fiery heart of Elohim. Michael was unsure but thought this had to have something to do with Man.

The Archangel stepped from the bridge to the floor. He purposefully kept his head and eyes down, not looking at the throne. He wanted to wait until he was directly in front of it.

He walked slowly, tears flowing from his eyes. Something overcame him, indeed, who could maintain composure in His presence?

He reached the center, in front of the great seat of the One, out from which the great river flowed. Still looking down, he could see the burning stones were between him and the throne. Each glowed a beautiful orange flame. Barely visible, the flames shot straight up in the air. *These flames must come from the very heart of Elohim.*

Slowly, he lifted his head, closed his eyes, and turned to face the throne. The heat flooded his face. He paused, not opening his eyes right away, savoring the moment.

His eyes opened slowly. He saw the Creator of All seated on the throne. His internal fire was plainly visible with his swirling clouds all around, emanating from the center. Never before had Michael been this close to the Creator, and the sight was completely overwhelming.

173

His knees buckled, his wings lurching from their position of rest in a vain effort to steady him. He hit the floor hard, knees first, then hands, then tumbled completely prostrate, wings still outstretched.

"OH MY ELOHIM!" His sobbing voice could be heard above all else in the throne room, "I AM NOTHING IN YOUR PRESENCE. YOU ARE SET APART FROM ALL CREATION! NONE IS LIKE YOU!" He lay there, his hands holding his face as he sobbed in the weighty presence of the Creator.

After quite a long time, he felt a large hand on his shoulder. Looking first one way, not seeing anything, then looking the other way, he saw the familiar feet of one of the Seraphim angels. Strength returned to him.

"Let me help you up," said the glowing dragon.

Once back on his feet, the seraphim, standing beside him placed his hand on Michael's back and called toward the throne, "Lord God Almighty, I present the archangel, guardian of your people, Michael, your humble servant!"

Michael had not expected to be introduced, he was not sure what he expected, he had come to simply *be* with Elohim before heading back to Earth.

"Welcome Michael, my good and faithful servant. I have been expecting you." Elohim spoke, with a cheerful voice.

*Expecting me? Of course He has been expecting me! This is Elohim after all!* His thoughts jumbled in the presence of his Creator.

"You are wrestling with limits and limitlessness, time and eternity. This will be your existence. As you travel back and forth between Paradise and Earth these differences will become easier for you and your choir to understand, at least in some measure." Elohim said. "You wondered as you walked on the bridge about the lamp stands." Michael nodded and Elohim continued. "Those are the seven spirits of Elohim. The lamp stands are both symbolic and literal. They *are* the seven spirits, while they cannot *contain* the seven spirits."

"Michael, in any reality that you can experience, I AM both there and yet not *contained*. You see a portion of Me here on the throne, yet on the throne is not where I AM completely. Do you understand?" Elohim asked.

"You are also on the Earth right now, are You not? I believe you exist everywhere, that everything that exists, is inside you. I have come to believe You are manifesting a portion of Yourself here, but it is only a portion. You are difficult to understand."

"Your insights into my existence are adequate for now," Elohim continued. "You wondered about these Seraphim. You were right in thinking my light is entering them, it is true. They are seeing aspects of me that have been revealed to no one else. I will continue to show them new and ever increasing wonders within myself as long as they wish to stay. These angels started as guards, not facing the throne; however, one turned and looked, as my Spirit worked within him. When he turned, I began to show him My glory, only a small portion, very small in fact. He began to praise Me for what I showed him, and I continued showing him more. His whispers of praise began to be heard faintly by the others, and eventually they turned to see what he was doing. That was when the other three turned to look.

Their whispers have been growing slowly and steadily as I show them more. You must understand, I do not show them more because they praise Me, I show them more because they desire to know Me more fully. Their praise to Me is not for my benefit, but for theirs. You will understand this more fully as your heart embraces me more and more, in an ever-expanding, all-encompassing endeavor."

Elohim paused for a moment, then continued, "What they did not understand when they were assigned to this detail was that I do not need guards in the sense of protection. No, they were assigned in their role of guards to *watch*, and now they understand. These four are able to see more now than they could when they first turned, and the measure they can endure will continue to increase, until My great and terrible day." Elohim spoke sternly in the voice of Thunder, the soft wind in the throne room became a torrent. Michael could, with great effort, stand in the midst of it. "On that day these four will be My witnesses, not My only witnesses mind you, but these will have a testimony of Me like no others."

"Michael, your angels are to watch over my people, and in this assignment they must travel throughout the Earth, to unlock the mysteries I have put there. You will find unusual things, and in those things lie mysteries. Mysteries that will help my people to understand my nature. You must also treat man as My representative, you must honor men as you honor Me, for when you honor them you are honoring Me."

Elohim concluded, "Michael, I love you, thank you for coming. Stay as long as you see fit."

Michael bowed before his creator and, looking more intently, could almost discern a form, a vague outline of a torso, arms and legs, and a head with a crown of light...then the form was gone, lost in the swirl of fire and clouds.

## Chapter 22

# Day Eleven

So many flying creatures. Two days would be devoted to naming them all. The tenth day Adam had spent naming the flying insects, and now, on the eleventh day, he would spend the entire day naming the flying mammals, birds, and reptiles.

He listened to the sound of the first tiny birds, "These will be called 'humming birds.'" Their sound and the blur of their wings made him smile. Two tiny birds landed on his hand. Both looked into his face, then one of the two tilted her head, studying him. Then she turned toward the Creator, gazed up at Him and bowed, and her companion joined her. Then the two looked back toward the man and bowed before flying away, weaving this way and that, in search of bright multi-colored flowers.

---

Lucifer flew over many large fires with winged beings huddled around them, some of them laughing, others engaged in serious talks, and still others peering silently into the darkness. Short blasts of flames erupted beneath him, piercing the darkness, adding to fires that had dimmed. Immense eerie tentacle-like spires jutted up from the ground, twisting their way high into the sky. Lucifer flew between the pillars, blasting fire at them to light his way. In the fire gleaming jewels were visible, protruding from the rough-hewn obelisks of the darkness. The surrounding rocks and mountains provided many places to hide from the view of others. Secrecy came to be something to relish, anonymity cherished. Below he could see the smoke of the dragons' burned breath which remained close to the ground, hanging in the air and lighted by the many fires, diffusing the light into an eerie glow.

He banked to the left and began the long journey to the portal that led to Earth. As he passed over their heads, many seraphim called out to him from below, cheering their commander, others blowing blasts of flame into the sky in salute. Flying lower now, smoke from the fires flowed off the tips of his wings in six circular vorticies followed by a great whooshing sound.

Flying through the Paradise portal, out the other side, the changes that had taken place in the darkness had become evident: his countenance had dimmed, the once shining red dragon was now more of a dark maroon color, with patches that were even darker.

Lucifer flew through Paradise toward the Earth portal and contemplated his new home. It may have been dark and cold, but he could also get away from the overwhelming presence of Elohim. He knew something was wrong with creation and he knew this man was at the center of the problem. He just had not assembled all the pieces of the puzzle yet.

His mission was an important one, for he had to be sure the reports he had received from his advisors were correct, and if so, he wanted to convince Michael concerning his position. This would be a bold move, but he felt confident that the Archangel would not only be able to answer his questions, but also, and more important, he hoped to lead the hosts of heaven as he once had done.

---

Michael circled, watching the Creator and the man as they named several kinds of birds. He began to understand what Elohim had said to him. *Being in creation, yet not contained.*

Adam saw a circling creature in the distance. He had seen these creatures before. Turning to Elohim he asked, "Will I be naming those?"

"No, Adam. Those already have a name: those are Cherubim, one type of angel. They were created in my realm, Paradise. You will learn more about them as time passes. The one you see there is called 'Michael,' and he and his entire company of angels are assigned to you."

"Assigned to me? What are they going to do?" the man asked.

"They are going to help you."

"What about the others I saw?" Adam asked. "I have seen this type before, and the others, that walk on four legs? What are they called?"

"Those are called Seraphim, and they are mighty dragons."

Just then a pair of brightly-colored birds flew to Adam, and came to rest on his outstretched arm.

Elohim turned the man's attention back to the task at hand.

"Ah ha! what have we here...?"

Adam thought for a moment. "These will be called... 'Parrots.'"

———————

Michael flew over the land, marveling at how beautiful it all was. Similar to Heaven. He wondered at how a small sprout could become a mature tree bearing fruit within just a few hours in the presence of the glory in which this man had been clothed. He marveled at the interplay of the light and shadows and how the Earth seemed to revolve through the light, the lush forests alternately resting and growing as they passed from darkness into light.

Slowly descending, he landed near a group of his angels. They saluted, a sign of respect.

"Gather the choir, we will come together here first thing tomorrow." Michael ordered.

"Yes sir!" The angels said as they departed.

As they left, another angel flew to him, landing several yards away with a salute. "Sir, Lucifer is here and asked me to find you. He would like to speak with you."

"Lucifer is here? Take me to him."

"This way sir." The messenger leapt into the air and Michael followed close behind.

———————

The two angels made their way along the green hills, over great rivers and streams, lakes and ponds. Passing over yet-unnamed creatures, the diversity never ceased to amaze Michael. The second angel motioned to his Archangel to follow him to the left. Michael nodded and the two banked as one. Just past a flock of Pterosaurs the second angel called to Michael, "Sir, he is right down there," and pointed in the direction of a large dark opening in the hillside.

"Where is he? I do not see him."

"He is in the cave, sir."

Michael called out, "Thank you! You are dismissed!" And he descended toward the cave as the other angel turned to head back.

---

The dark figure heard the familiar sound of feathers outside the cave opening and called out, "In here! Michael, I am in here!"

Hearing his former commander, he used his mighty wings to lift himself to the mouth of the cave and stepped in, folding his plumage behind him. A puzzled look came over his face as he walked into the darkness of the cave. He moved ahead to a flickering light in the distance. In the shadows he saw movement and wondered why Lucifer would want to meet here, in the dark.

---

The tallest of the Archangels by a good six to eight inches, at thirteen feet tall the handsome and powerfully built Michael approached. His demeanor was one of controlled strength, and there was an elegance about his movements. In his countenance there was a light or radiance, golden in color and barely perceptible. His skin was golden and his long hair covered the top of his silver-colored armor breastpiece. His sword hung on his left hip and his movements were full of grace and humility as he slung his shield onto his back, covering part of his now-resting wings. His fiery blue eyes revealed the intensity of the flame within.

---

"Michael!" his former Commander's eyes brightened a little as the cherubim walked closer, "It is good to see you."

Michael picked up his pace, and when he arrived in front of Lucifer, he saluted. The dragon returned the salute, placed a hand on Michael's shoulder, a sly smile on his face, "Thank you for coming."

Michael's nerves were eased at once. His Commander had always inspired confidence. "Of course! You needed to see me, Sir?"

"Please, don't call me *sir*. I am not your Commander anymore! That was only for the preparation time. You have your own assignment now, and I have mine. We are equals, brothers."

Michael pondered this thought for a moment. "Brothers, hmmm, I never thought of it like that before. I suppose you are right. I am glad you came and I am glad to see you! Would you like to look around? The Creator is not far from here with the Man, would you like to see what they are doing today?"

"No! I mean...thank you, not right now." Lucifer's eyes were diverted to the cave opening, "I appreciate your hospitality, but I really came to speak only with you. Please come and sit with me."

Michael sensed the importance in his former Commander's tone and sat on a large flat rock next to the fire. "What did you need to see me about?"

"Michael, I have a growing concern about this creation, this Earth." He paused, blew more fire to bolster the depleting flames, then took a couple of steps back in order to sit down while wrapping his tail around his front feet. The serrated horns at the end of the dragon's tail seemed longer and sharper than Michael had remembered, and the blades gleamed in the fire light. "Everything seemed fine until Elohim created this... Man."

"I do not understand." Michael had never heard anyone question Elohim before. "What do you mean?"

"This man is made to look like Elohim, right?" Lucifer asked.

"Right."

"I have reports that the creatures will occasionally bow to this man."

"That is right, it happens all the time," Michael confirmed.

Lucifer rose to his feet, turned from Michael and asked "How can they bow to any except Elohim?"

"Elohim wants us to honor the man, just as we honor Him."

"What?" Lucifer turned back to face Michael, and his puzzled expression had changed to anger. His eyes glowed yellow in the darkness.

Michael continued warily, "He told me the man is His ambassador to this world, and as such, when we honor him we are honoring Elohim."

Lucifer's countenance softened as his brow line raised and his mouth opened slightly. He stood in silence, eyes moving back and forth as he thought, and the tip of his tail tapped the cave floor. "I do not understand. Man is made of clay; we are made of fire and water." He paused again, some part of his being that had begun closing days earlier, now closed completely, crusting over, hardening. "I will not bow to this...*Man*! I am better than he!"

Michael rose to his feet. He had to try to get through to the dragon, get him to obey, make him understand! Before he could say a word, Lucifer lunged for the cave opening. His wings roared in the enclosed space, and then he disappeared from view.

Michael stood in silence for several seconds, took a deep breath, and headed back out the way he came.

---

The four had gathered, searching in the west for some sort of entrance to this mystery location the seraphim had talked about. After hours of searching, the four sat on a hill talking about where they might look next.

A huge black object shot over their heads. Each of them ducked, their flames following the direction of this very fast object. As it continued on, they noticed the six black leathery wings.

"Let us go!" called Hillel as he took to the sky in pursuit.

The other three, without a word caught up with him.

"Hang back a bit, do not get too close." Kalil said to the others.

Several miles separated them from the one they pursued, when all of a sudden the dark dragon banked to the right and down, looking as though he had crashed into the ground at full speed, dust flying into the air.

---

"This one will be called, "Hawk" and these over here will be called, "Eagle." The man continued his work, as the Creator looked on.

"One more to go," Elohim said as he whisked Adam to the northernmost part of the single land mass and sat him down. The little birds waddled toward the man, colored in black and white. Adam looked at them, "Penguin is what you shall be called."

The little penguins bowed to both of them and scampered off to the water's edge. They plunged into the ocean, flying through the water as elegantly as the other birds flew through the air.

---

The four slowed as they came closer to the place where their target had disappeared. The grassy ground ended at a canyon's edge, and the canyon wound around, cliff walls on both sides. They looked at each other, realizing they could not stop looking now.

"Spread out." Hillel could not believe the Commander had escaped their view so easily. "We have a good chance of finding the entrance since we know he turned to the right in this area." Hillel studied the place where apparently the dragon had struck the ground hard with his tail, tearing a portion of the cliff wall loose.

## Chapter 23

# Day Twelve

Like a cannon ball through the barrel of a mortar, Lucifer shot through the tunnel. The cyclonical wind, generated as he flew, flung slower dragons onto the tunnel walls. His rage had only grown since leaving the small cave on earth and all he could think about was getting back to the Crypsis. His vision had narrowed to this one mission, RETURN. He could think of nothing else. All else was anger, so full of it was he that every exhalation was fire, and his eyes lighted the cave before him in a bath of pale yellow light.

----

Fires were burning all around, like large camp fires, and dragons crouched around them, talking amongst themselves, or just sitting quietly.

Semyaza and Azazel spoke in quiet tones.

Semyaza blew more flames into the fire. "Do you think the Commander's talk with Michael will help calm him somewhat?"

"I hope so." Azazel paused. "You know, I agree with him. There are many things we do not understand, that do not make sense."

---

Lucifer could contain it no more: his anger flooded from his body in a tortured resonant shriek. The walls of the cave burst into flame before him. He emerged onto the dark expanse, piercing the flames that now encompassed the opening, his six wings roared and strained under the muscular contractions that beat the air as never before, portions of them carrying bits of flame from the tunnel.

The two generals were startled by the shriek from the cave above them. Their attention was torn from the warmth of their fire, to the cave opening. They saw Lucifer just as he passed the first of the towering pillars, smashing the top with his tail. The pinnacle broke off and tumbled down to the ground. Several dragons below moved an instant before it came crashing down where they had been, snuffing out their fire.

Semyaza broke the murky silence, "I guess Michael was unable to help."

"No, I think it is worse now. Come on, let us go talk to him."

"Let us not be hasty. Maybe we should let him calm down a little first."

Azazel thought for a moment, "Yes, maybe you are right." He blew on the fire and watched it grow taller between them.

---

"Adam, today will be the last day that you will be naming animals," the Creator said. "Today you will be naming the creatures that walk on the surface and under the surface of the land. Are you ready?"

"Ready," Adam answered, as he saw the first of these creatures making their way to them.

---

Michael's choir gathered. The Archangel struggled to put the ordeal with Lucifer behind him so he could give his troops the Creator's instructions.

"Hosts of Heaven," Michael began, "I spoke with the Creator, and I have further instructions that will enable us to fulfill His will. All of us have been tasked with searching out the mysteries of earth, all the various things. Elohim has hidden knowledge of Himself all around us. These things must be discovered, and in the course of time, we will discover them, in the waters, the vast lands, and under the lands. Every type of living thing holds mysteries, and at the appointed time, we must be prepared to help man in discovering them. We are also called upon to honor this man and protect him from anything that might try to harm him."

The massive group of angels began to stir. Murmurs wove through the crowd. One angel pushed to the front of the group. "Sir, may I ask a question?"

"Of course, what is it?"

"Who would try to harm Man? The creatures here on earth, in the sea, the lakes, rivers, in the air or on the ground, all of the animals as with the host of heaven revere the man because of the attention Elohim has shown him. What danger could possibly exist?"

"I have been told by one with more authority than I, that there are those whose choices have pulled them from Elohim's path. I believe this means that the goodness we know will be changing somehow, and you will be called upon to protect Man. This can only happen if protection is needed, so in all you do, stay diligent to the tasks at hand. Help and protect the man from whatever threatens him. We were made for this."

The angel spoke again. "Yes sir, may we fulfill the command of Elohim." Pulling his sword from its sheath, he turned to the group of angels behind him and yelled, "TO SERVE AND PROTECT!"

The sound of hundreds of millions of swords escaping their bonds and bursting into flame as they were thrust overhead could be heard as the throng of angels answered back, "TO SERVE AND PROTECT!"

———————

Lucifer paced back and forth, smoke belching from his nostrils as he fought to contain this explosive anger. Power coursed through his veins, and those around him cowered at this new posture he had taken on.

Azazel approached Commander Lucifer, "Sir, can you tell us what has happened? We sent patrols out when you returned to give us a report. They have all returned without finding anything out of the ordinary."

The Commander grabbed Azazel by the throat, looked directly into his eyes and asked, "Who do you bow your knee to, General?"

"I bow to the Creator, and Him only," Azazel answered without wavering.

"Right," Lucifer said indignantly, releasing his hold on the general, "The Creator wants you to bow to *Man!* He wants you to bow to the clay image of Himself."

"This cannot be! Are you sure?" Another general asked.

"I am sure. Michael told me himself." Turning to the gathering crowd of dragons, he shouted, "We do not bow to any but Elohim! I don't care if this man is the Creator's little project, I will not honor him as I have honored Elohim. I will not do it!"

Azazel turned to the crowd of Seraphim who had heard fragments of the discussion and were moving toward them. "I am with you, Commander Lucifer."

The General began chanting to the troops, "We will not bow, We will not bow!" Soon the entire group of Seraphim joined in. Huge kettle drums began pounding out the rhythm, and many of the dragons began dancing to the beat and the chanting. Whooping and yelling, they danced in circles around their fires and blew more fire high into the air in sync with the droning beat.

––––––––

"What is that?" Malkiel froze.

"What?"

"Listen!"

The other three gathered around Malkiel, and they were completely quiet except for the slight undulation of their flames.

"We will not what?" asked Ozel.

Hillel looked at the other three, "I cannot make it out, there is too much other noise."

Kalil closed his eyes, and concentrated on the commotion. "Bow...they said, We will not bow," came his response.

"What do you think *that* means?" Hillel asked the others.

———————

The cave darkened even more as the hearts of all the occupants, now rejecting the wishes of their King in favor of their Commander, began to close, sealing shut and crusting over, concealing the light. Once sealed, the flames within their hearts were snuffed out. Almost every seraphim in attendance became dark, like their leader. Millions of yellow eyes glowed in the darkness.

———————

As the line of land creatures neared the end, at least in this location, Adam looked up to Elohim "You made me in your image, did you not?"

"Yes, that is right."

Adam glanced back again to the animals. "Each of these animals has a match..."

"Yes..."

"But *I* am not made like them."

"That is right."

Adam looked back to his Creator, as a tear collected at the inside corner of his eye and spilled over, down his face, as this new realization flowed through his heart.

"This one," Adam said, wiping his face, "you will be called 'Lamb.' Your coat resembles our Creator's billowing outer layer, you are blessed to have His appearance, and yet, you have a counterpart."

———————

The four found Uriel, who had been instructing several from his troop on how to achieve greater speed. The four stood about fifteen yards from the Archangel, waiting for a good moment to approach him.

Uriel glanced in their direction, then turned to his pupils and told them to take a break. He dismissed himself and walked over to the four. They could not help but notice that his flames were now pure blue. He welcomed them. "I see by your coloring that you four have figured out some of what it takes to fly fast." He gave them an approving nod.

The four spoke in unison, "Yes sir."

"Very good. Did you need to see me? Looks as if the four of you have something on your minds."

"Umm, Yes Sir," Hillel began, "well, sir, I had noticed, that is, we had noticed. Let me start again: we noticed that the seraphim had all disappeared..."

"Except for the ones at the throne room..." interrupted Malkiel.

"Right, except for those. Not those. But the rest are nowhere to be found." Hillel continued.

"Calm down, no need to be nervous," Uriel tried to calm Hillel's nerves while motioning for Malkiel to let him continue.

"We found a cave, and we think they are all in it..." Hillel explained.

"Must be a large cave." Uriel spoke his thoughts.

"Yes sir, we did overhear them call it the Crypsis, though I am not sure if that means anything," Hillel responded.

Uriel paused, then leaned toward them, "You four stay here, I am going to finish up with these angels, then I want you to take me to this cave you found."

The Archangel walked back to his pupils, "All right, let us try again. You need to let the power out! You cannot try to hang on to it and expect it to do any good! Be a river, not a lake. The power must flow through, do not stop it up!" The orange flaming angels were trying to figure it out, zooming this way and that, little by little gaining more speed.

The four angels felt relieved that soon Uriel would know as much as they did.

Ozel spoke to his companions quietly, "Uriel will know how to handle this."

---

The assembly had just ended, and each team of angels headed to a different portion of the Earth. During the meeting one of the attendants noticed something was troubling the Archangel. Walking over to Michael, he asked, "Sir, are you all right?"

Michael glanced toward him, "I am not sure, but something is happening to Lucifer; something is not right. He is acting very strangely, and his appearance is different...he looked darker, as if a shadow had fallen over him, or maybe it was the cave's darkness I was seeing."

"What do you think it is?" The attendant asked.

"I do not know, but I have never heard anyone talk the way he was talking. He seemed completely devoted to Elohim, and in the same breath, not." Michael said.

"Not devoted to the Creator? How can that be?"

"I do not know. It does not make any sense. Keep this between us for now. I am going to go find the Man, to see how he is doing with naming everything." Michael lifted from the ground and flew in the direction where he believed the man and Elohim were.

"Yes sir," the attendant said, to the space where Michael had been.

---

This one shall be called, "Rhinoceros," and this one shall be called, "Elephant." Tears flowing down as his thoughts were torn between naming the animals and grasping the understanding of just how alone Elohim was. Looking around, again wiping the tears from his eyes, the man looked for more creatures to name. None came. He looked up to his Creator and Elohim said to him, "You have named all of the creatures."

Adam paused, looked away from his Creator, toward the horizon, saw the clouds, the birds flying in the distance, and heard the lapping of a lake near by. "It is not good for Elohim to be alone."

All of mankind now echoed the sentiment of his Creator, adding, "It is WRONG for Elohim to be alone!"

Adam walked a short distance to the edge of the hill, amazed at the view, the lush green of the grass, bushes and trees responding with astounding growth from the light given off by the man and even more so the light of the Creator. The growth was evident as Adam watched. Indeed, everywhere they had gone, into the sea, or anywhere on the Earth, whenever they were present the surrounding plants responded with rapid growth, producing seed and fruit according to their kind.

Sighing deeply, the man said, "It is terribly wrong for Elohim to be alone."

The last thing the man heard before everything went black on the Twelfth day, came from behind him. The booming, thunderous voice of the almighty Elohim declaring, "It is not good for man to be alone!" Adam fell to the ground, in a deep sleep.

---

"His emotion runs very deep." One angel watching the proceeding said to the other.

"Very deep," said the other in response, "much like his Creator."

"Yes."

The two watched, part of a small group of only several thousand cherubim, as Elohim opened the Man's side. Blood and water began flowing out as he removed a section of flesh and bone. Then He closed the place, purposefully leaving a wound where he had worked. He moved with the quickness of light several miles away to finish this great work.

He worked with great care, and careful precision in the presence of Michael, and several Cherubim from Michael's choir Katriel, Leibel, and Feivel.

"Elohim?"

"Yes, Michael," the Creator answered tenderly.

"What are you doing?"

"I am forming a bride."

Several moments passed before Michael again spoke, "What is bride?"

"A counterpart for man." Elohim said as he steadily worked, his hands smoothing the new flesh into a shape similar to the Man, though the differences were evident.

"The other creatures counterparts do not have an appearance this different from one another." Michael noted.

"I created them all, but not this one. This one must be formed from him. She will share his flesh and bone and blood and spirit," Elohim responded, finishing the last curve. They watched as her hair grew out quickly. The glory she was clothed in would bathe the surroundings, outside the presence of the Creator, giving her a very similar appearance to that of the Man.

"Michael, gather as many of the angelic host to the skies above the divide as can attend," Elohim said. "Tomorrow a glorious event will take place, and I want you all to witness it. You have several hours before morning, and I want to start just as the sun rises, so you better get moving."

"We will be ready!"

---

Sometime during the night the four creatures had again heard something in the surrounding stadium. All four turned at once, again urged to do so by the Spirit of Elohim. Another bright-white being appeared and was seated next to the first. Now, there were two.

# Chapter 24

# *Day Thirteen*

Michael sent for his angels during the night, as Elohim formed this counterpart for Man. Elohim wanted the angels, at least the ones who did not have other duties, to attend this first-time event. As with the creation of man, the angels gathered for this presentation.

The grass-covered pathway was long and straight, lined with every kind of fruit tree, all in blossom. The sky was blue with a few stratus clouds to give a touch of variety. Birds filled the trees, and a vast variety of animals populated the path between the trees.

Just before sunrise, Michael touched the man on his shoulder, reviving him. Giving Adam his hand, the Archangel helped the man to his feet, brushing off his back. Adam felt a sharp twinge of pain from his side and with his left hand touched the spot under his clothing woven of light. The place was more than a little tender.

Tracing the edge of the wound with his fingers, he wondered what it was. He pulled his hand away, his finger tips wet, stained red.

Just then, Michael gently turned him toward the path. It seemed that Elohim was at the opposite end, with a smaller light beside him, the sun's light breaking over the horizon rising behind them both. Confused, he asked Michael, "What is this?"

Michael pressed his finger to his lips, then pointed for Adam to look back down the path. Michael stood with him, waiting as Elohim walked the counterpart of man down the path. The birds all sang the same song, the very same song the angels were singing.

---

Lucifer and his dragons arrived just before the ceremony started, and stayed behind the other angels. They were all fascinated to see what was about to take place. Lucifer's countenance had grown darker still, while his skin had begun to form plates, matching the crust on his heart. The plates covered the jewels that had been set into his skin, concealing them. He seemed to be hiding behind walls his own body had constructed.

---

As Elohim drew closer, the Man's focus shifted to the smaller light next to him. This one was covered in white light, just as he was. The birds watched her walk by and they too noticed her movements were different. She seemed much more graceful than the Man. Her covering of light seemed to trail behind her like a garment, her face veiled, and her hair flowing like liquid onyx down her back.

As the fog of his deep sleep subsided, Adam realized what was happening: Elohim was presenting one more creature for him to name. This one, much different from the others, was like him. "How can this be?" Adam's thoughts wrestled their way out of him. He searched for the answer, all the while watching this new one coming down the pathway. His side began hurting again, and again he touched the wound, realizing where this new counterpart had come from. "This one came from my body?" he asked, looking at Michael. The Archangel, eyes focused ahead, gave a slight nod in agreement, a small smile on his face.

Elohim and this new counterpart approached Adam. Elohim stopped a few yards back and motioned for the smaller one to continue forward, while He announced, "Adam, I give you your counterpart."

Adam stepped to her, taking her hand. The light veiling her face cleared slightly, and he looked into her eyes, knowing now she was made from his flesh. He expected to see his own expression somehow. He expected her to look like himself, thought he would see the same face as he had seen in his reflection in the water.

She was not at all what he expected-she was beautiful. The hard, ruddy lines smoothed, the shape of her eyes somehow different. Her appearance literally took his breath away. He had never breathed this hard in his life! He began to lose his balance, gravity lost its direction, his eyes lost their focus, and his body began to sink to the ground. The emotions of the moment, his wound, and the fog of so recently being unconscious all caught up with him in this vital moment. The archangel responded quickly, grabbing Adam's shoulders, literally keeping him from toppling over. The archangel poured strength into Adam as he held him up, and a look of concern covered the angel's face.

---

The flaming Archangel glanced over to Lucifer, noting the difference in his countenance. Having seen the cave entrance, he was curious to find out what was happening with his former leader. He wondered how the Commander and most, if not all, of his troops' appearances had changed, or continued to change. What could be causing this?

Lucifer's eyes began to move back and forth slightly, suddenly aware of Uriel's stare. Looking over in the Archangel's direction, Lucifer nodded slightly. Uriel returned the greeting, tipping his head up and looking back toward the ceremony.

———————

Adam, his strength recovered, in no small part because of Michael, stepped directly in front of his newly-formed counterpart, and said "This one is called 'Woman,' because she was taken out of man."

Woman asked, "...and what shall I call you?" Her delicate feminine voice spoke for the first time.

The man paused, closed his eyes, soaking in her sound. Then opening his eyes once again responded, "My name is Adam."

"Woman, do you take this man as your counterpart?" Elohim asked.

She could feel the deep desire of her Creator, knowing the loneliness man had felt over the past few days, having already experienced them while she was a part of Adam. All the emotions of that moment crowding in, she knew that while this would solve the dilemma for themselves, it would not fulfill the desire of the Creator. She looked to the one who formed her, sensing His pleasure in this ceremony, His voice within her saying "Please, take this gift I give to you."

"I do." She responded with a gentle smile, a tear rolling down her face.

The finger of Elohim touched her cheek, wiping the tear away. She thought she could see a smile, that His heart was glad.

Michael moved once again to stand beside Adam, having strengthened him sufficiently, at least for the moment.

"Adam, do you take this woman as your bride, your counterpart?" Elohim asked.

Adam looked a sight as tears flowed down his face, his nose running, his eyes very sad, glancing this way and that, then back to the Creator of all. "What about *you*?" Adam asked. "Where's your counterpart?"

"Adam, she must be formed, and she is being formed." Elohim replied.

"Why should you have to wait?" Adam said under his breath, then louder, "You should not have to wait!"

"I will wait, and she is worth the wait." Elohim replied. "I AM establishing an order here today, this ceremony is important, so please, Adam, accept my gift to you."

Adam wiped his face and tried, almost in vain, to smile. Elohim was again giving him an amazing gift, this one far greater than the others. He nodded his head several times quickly, "All right, can we try again?"

"Adam," Elohim repeated "do you take this woman as your bride, your counterpart?"

Adam turned back to the woman, tears streaming down her face as she turned her gaze back from Elohim to Adam. Their eyes met as she heard Adam say, "I do."

And what was separated for a time was once again brought together. After a short pause, lightning broke out all around them as Elohim thundered with delight, "You may kiss the bride!"

The man and the woman, looked to each other. Both of their faces wet with tears of simultaneous sadness and joy. Sad for their friend, their Creator, but also joyful, knowing they would never be alone again, and the Creator would have His bride. Adam leaned forward, Woman responded, and the two kissed, eyes closed as a tingling sensation rushed throughout their bodies. The warmth of the moment was indeed meant to be savored, and savor it they did. The kiss lingered for many moments until each very slowly pulled away, eyes remaining closed. Opening their eyes at last, each looked into the eyes of the other, their hearts full of intense joy.

----

Lucifer knew something profound had just happened, but his anger blinded his mind to such a degree that he could not grasp this new event fully. He left the ceremony as soon as it had finished. The thunder all around him concealed his departure and that of his seraphim followers. His rage having been fueled further by this formal joining of man and the woman, something that had not happened with the other earth creatures. He needed to discuss this with some of his generals; surely they could focus better at this point than he could. As his choir followed behind, he flew toward the cave where he had talked to Michael. It was a smaller place where he could have a private meeting with his generals.

As they approached their destination, he looked over to Azazel, "You and the rest of the generals, follow me, and send the rest of the troops back to the Crypsis to wait for us."

"As you wish!" Azazel called out as he turned to locate the other generals.

---

Two purple-blue flames managed to go unnoticed as they followed the generals to the Earth cave. They watched through the trees as several of the generals made a roaring fire in the clearing just outside the cave. Darkness was setting in and all the generals huddled, rubbing their hands together, waiting for the rest of the generals to show up.

Azazel grew frustrated, "Where's Semyaza?"

One of the others spoke up, "I do not know, I did not see him. I thought he was already here."

Then another spoke. "I saw him, he was speaking with some of the other angels."

Azazel turned toward the cave, "Let us go, we cannot keep Lucifer waiting." The generals filed two or three at a time into the cave's opening.

Hillel began approaching, easing closer, weaving his way among the trees, keeping behind them as much as possible.

"What are you doing? They're going to see you!" Kalil's desperation was apparent.

"No, they are not, come with me. We have to get closer to find out what is happening, we were sent here to find out, not to look from a distance. Now come on!" Hillel's whispers urged Kalil to follow along, however reluctantly.

The two spies made their way to the edge of the clearing before the cave, then pointing to the large fire in the center, said, "That looks to me like a good hiding place, think we can both fit?"

"Our flames are blue, that fire is orange." Kalil's eyes opened wide as he watched his friend slowly change to an orange color.

Hillel whispered, "Restrict the flow of power, remember?"

"Remember? What are you talking about? How did you do that?"

"Remember when Uriel was teaching the troops to fly faster?"

"Yes."

"He said they needed to learn to let the power flow through them, and faster means bluer, right?

"Right"

"So restrict the power, until the color is right..."

Kalil's color began to change until he more or less matched his friend.

Both moved together, keeping low to the ground, the elevated floor of the cave concealed them. Entering the fire, each began adjusting their orange flames to better match the fire all around them.

Hillel heard something approaching and looking behind them, he saw one of the Generals nearing.

"Kal, crouch down."

Kalil looked down to see Hillel already squatting. "What?"

"Crouch down, we have company."

Kalil squatted down with Hillel just before Semyaza moved from the thick foliage and into the clearing. In one swift movement he leapt up to the cave entrance and proceeded into the darkness.

The two spies slowly rose and peered into the cave, straining to see or hear what was happening.

———————

"Sir, I am not sure how we can say there was much to it, other than Elohim wanting to make a big deal out of creating the mate for the man. All the animals were made in pairs, and now we know the man is just like the rest." said one of the generals.

"Commander, that is not right." Semyaza pushed his way to the front of the group as he spoke.

"Semyaza, so you've finally arrived?" Lucifer, sneering, asked with much interest.

"I am sorry, Sir, I was late because I waited to speak with two angels from Michael's choir."

"And what did you learn?"

"Turns out that Elohim did not create the female after all."

Azazel could not believe it, "What? How is that possible?"

"Elohim, as it turns out, formed the woman from flesh taken from the man."

Another General countered, "This cannot be!"

"The man still has the wound."

Azazel held up his hand toward the second General and asked, "Elohim removed part of the man to make something else?"

"That is correct."

Lucifer interjected, "See, I knew there must be something wrong with Man. He removed the best part and made the woman!"

———————

Two more blue dots followed the massive hoard of dragons heading back to the Crypsis. These two, one larger than the other, could stay farther back, since the entrance to the dark world was no longer a mystery.

———————

The blue-flamed Archangel approached Michael. Giving the customary salute of greeting and respect as he folded his wings behind him, Uriel began to chuckle, "Greetings Captain, you had your hands full back there!"

Michael's eyebrows rose, a slight laugh escaping as he shook his head. "Hold on for a while, I need to speak with you."

"I figured I would let the crowd thin out, but I need to speak with you as well." Each of them waited to speak with the other and this would be an opportune time. The crowd continued to thin, until finally the two Archangels were in effect alone.

"Captain, did you notice Lucifer in the crowd?" Uriel asked.

"No, I did not. Did you see him?"

"I did, he arrived late and left as soon as it was over. I have to tell you though, I almost did not recognize him."

"Yes, I saw him a couple of days ago. He looked different all right. Although when I saw him it was dark, and we were only illuminated by a fire."

"I do not know what you saw, but what I saw today was beyond 'different'" Uriel said with a note of urgency.

Michael turned to look directly at him. "How so?"

"His entire countenance was darkened, not a color, more as if his skin were constantly in a shadow. Oh, and his skin is covered over with some sort of heavy plating."

"I do not know what was causing it... However, he seemed to be having a hard time with man when I last saw him."

"Man?" A puzzled look invaded Uriel's face.

"He was very upset that Elohim seems to favor the Man."

"Why?"

"I do not know, something about man being beneath him, and he does not believe we should obey the Creator in how we treat Man, and now there are two of them," Michael said.

"Do you think that has something to do with his appearance?"

"I am not sure. We should meet with Metatron, and let him know what is happening. He will probably know how to handle it. When you are back in Paradise, will you make plans with Metatron?"

"Yes, and I will send word on when you need to be there." The two exchanged salutes, and Uriel roared into the sky, leaving Michael to marvel at his speed.

---

Adam lead his bride from the ceremony. Hand in hand, everything blooming as they walked. The clothing of light Elohim had provided them caused their surroundings to be like an immense garden, as though they worked and tilled the ground merely by being there.

Elohim watched the Man, seeing what it must be like to finally have a counterpart, knowing that this ceremony was but a foreshadowing of what was to come.

---

One of the generals noticed something peculiar about the fire outside. He was unsure what was bothering him, but he kept glancing in the direction of the cave's opening to look at it.

Another General whispered, "Have you noticed it too?"

"Something about that fire bothers me," offered the first.

"It is not dying down, the flames remain as strong as when we came in here."

"Yes, that is it… Do you think flames stay strong longer here than in the Crypsis?"

"I do not know for sure, but I guess it is possible."

———————

"They are talking about Man, something about the ceremony. It does not sound as if they like anything about what just happened," Hillel said, straining to hear.

Kalil replied, "They surely do not sound happy, that is certain. I cannot really…"

"Wait a minute, do not move," Hillel interrupted.

Kalil broke the pause, whispering, "What is it?"

"Two of the generals are looking this way."

"How can you tell? I cannot see…"

"I can just make out their eyes. Look carefully, they are yellow…"

"Oh, I see now, two of them are looking toward us, I think we need to get out of here, they are moving, are they not?"

"I cannot be sure…No, wait, wait, yes, they are moving this way." Hillel was positive.

"Now what do we do? We cannot leave while they are watching."

"Wait to see if they look away, and if they do, then we will have a chance. Just stick with me."

———————

The generals proceeded slowly. Their movements drew the attention of several other generals, and one pointed them out to

Lucifer who addressed them directly, "Halloo! You two! We are trying to have a meeting here!" The Commander called out.

"Sorry, Sir. We were just noticing that the fire is not dying down outside." The first general pointed to the cave entrance.

"Really?" Lucifer's eyes squinted as he peered toward the opening.

"Yes, Sir. We thought that was strange and wanted to have a look," the first general continued. "Sorry for the interruption."

———————

"This is bad. This is really really bad. We cannot let them find us." Hillel whispered.

"What do we do? They are all looking!" Kalil began to panic.

———————

Lucifer rose to his feet, studying the fire outside. The rest of the group turned their attention to the blaze.

———————

"They are all looking this way. All of them are definitely looking this way now. They are going to find us!" Kalil's whispers began to sound much more intense.

"Wait a minute, just calm down."

"Calm down? How am I supposed to calm down?"

———————

Lucifer slowly began taking steps toward the fire outside, the generals following closely behind. Fifty yards, and they would be on top of the two flaming cherubim.

———————

"This is bad, bad, bad. All of them are coming this way now! If they find us, what are we going to say... 'We just wanted to stand in this fire for a while and find out what you were talking about?'" Kalil's voice began to rise, his whispers growing louder.

"Keep your voice down," Hillel scolded.

———————

In the darkness one of the dragons stumbled a bit, the tunnel was too small for the arrangement of dragons to fit comfortably. The slight stumble caused them all to look back in the direction of the misstep...

———————

This was just the break they needed. Hillel desperately whispered "GO!" Grabbing Kalil's arm, he released all the energy he could. An explosion of flame thrust the two into the air, and they began banking quickly to level off over the dense forest, the lush trees obscuring any view of them. Then quickly he again banked, still dragging Kalil around one of the mountain ridges.

———————

An explosion of flame roared behind the dragons as they looked away. They swung back to the entrance, startled by the sudden explosion of energy. Lucifer was first to emerge from the entrance, swooping down next to the flames, looking for clues as to what just happened. Azazel climbed into the air, assumed a high orbit, peering out to check for anything unusual, but he saw nothing that offered any explanation.

"I am not sure what just happened, Sir. I do not see anything strange, and the fire seems to be dying down now," Semyaza reported.

"All right, let us wrap it up here, we will head back." Lucifer stared at the fire, which had indeed become very small in the few minutes since they had left the cave.

———————

Outside the entrance to the Crypsis, Ozel and Malkiel prepared to head back to camp. Nothing was happening, and they needed to report in. Sabbath was upon them and they knew they needed to get back before the time of rest was upon them. As they prepared to leave, they heard the flapping of leathery wings, and it was growing louder, approaching. The two hid themselves the best they could in the rocks. The nine Seraphim flew toward them and banked away to the left, away from their view, and into the cave entrance without noticing the two at all. As the dragons vanished into the cave, the two Cherubim took to the sky and headed back to camp. Uriel would be waiting for their report.

## Chapter 25

# Day Fourteen

The man and the woman spent the day enjoying the good Earth Elohim had created. Walking through the lush garden that seemed to manifest its beauty wherever they traveled. The two walked hand in hand, mile after mile, not realizing the distance they were covering. The grass was so thick that their feet scarcely touched the ground, as if they were walking on a cloud. Occasionally, they paused to sample fruit from trees as they passed, apples and plums, oranges, pears, peaches, and huckleberries, all ripe with scents so rich they could almost be tasted before they bit into them.

They walked fingers intertwined, looking at the various animals. The Lion, whose mane as it moved with the wind reminded Woman of the flames of Elohim. This magnificent animal approached them, bowing his head in honor. Adam approached the majestic animal, running his hands through the lion's mane, Woman paying equal attention to the lioness.

Then the sheep also approached, bowing in respect.

---

Michael arrived just after Uriel, gliding down to stand on the balcony next to his friend.

Metatron sat at his desk, studying a parchment in front of him. He held his quill, and as he silently recited what he read, his pen bounced up and down, following along. Then all at once the scribe stopped, set his quill down and looked up to see the two waiting Archangels. He slowly rose to his feet. Leaning over the desk he glanced once more at the parchment, then shook his head and stood upright. "I am working on a puzzle of sorts, called the tetragrammaton."

"The tetra... what?"

"The tetragrammaton. Elohim's name is spelled three different ways: one way has four letters, the second has twelve letters, and the last has seventy-two letters. Now here is the interesting part: there are no vowels in any of the three spellings."

"How is anything pronounced without vowels?"

"That is the point, the names are not pronounceable. They are not definable either, at least at this point. I am working on figuring out the puzzle, assuming it is a puzzle." Metatron smiled and stepped away from his desk to face the two archangels, "How may I help you two?"

Uriel spoke first. "At the ceremony, Lucifer looked different, darker, and seemed to have some sort of plates growing from his skin. I could not see the jewels that normally adorn him."

Michael followed Uriel's lead. "And sir, I spoke with him on Earth, and his behavior was strange as well. He wanted to meet with me in a dark cave, so we talked around a fire. He was agitated with the importance that Elohim has placed in Man."

Metatron paused for a moment, listening, then with a nod he began, "I know this has raised your concerns. Lucifer has become something he never intended to become. He believes he is being perfectly reasonable, questioning everything. He is questioning Elohim, being skeptical, placing evil where it has never existed, and thereby taking evil into himself. He is allowing his choices to take him into the very thing he at one time could not imagine. He no longer trusts Elohim completely."

"What?" The archangels turned to look at each other, shaking their heads. "Not Lucifer, he is our mentor. We look up to him!"

A look of concern grew on Michael's face as he turned back to Metatron. "He does not trust the Creator?"

"No, he only trusts himself. He now believes he alone can protect himself," Metatron answered.

"Is this the struggle you spoke to me about, the difficult time that was coming?" Michael asked.

"Yes, you needed to face Lucifer's rage in that cave. You had to make your choice, and you have, both of you have," Metatron said. "Lucifer believes Elohim is flawed, and if the Creator is flawed, then all of creation is flawed, and in such a case, he will seek to overthrow the Creator."

"I think I understand," the golden haired archangel added, "What happens now?"

With a grim look Metatron stated flatly, "War."

———————

Lucifer motioned for the generals to stay together as they flew out of the portal and into the Crypsis. Climbing high, the group traveled just above the great stoney peaks, the millions of fires dotting the ground beneath them, each surrounded by dragons. Clearing the spires, the group came upon a large open area, framed on two sides with high cliffs jutting up into the air. Lucifer led the group to the top of the right side of the cliffs. Their eyes had grown accustomed to the dark during their times of exposure to the Crypsis, and in the blackness, they could now see shapes and some details, still nothing comparable to being in full light, but they no longer needed fire to navigate the surroundings.

"Bring all the dragons here quickly to this clearing. I want to address them all," Lucifer ordered.

---

Kalil, Hillel, Ozel and Malkiel waited just over the ridge from the Crypsis portal. They looked in the direction of the temple for any glimpse of Michael or Uriel leaving the meeting. Hillel paced slowly, then turning his head toward the cliff he heard the sound millions of wings make when moving in a swarm.

---

Metatron, his back now turned to the Archangels said, "You both need to inform the other archangels to be prepared. All of the angelic hosts are to meet in the throne room before midday. Get them assembled in full dress."

Michael and Uriel answered together, "Yes sir."

"Dismissed."

---

The sound of the dragons flying reminded him of rushing fluid, like a mighty water fall. Lucifer watched as the millions of dark wings flew toward him, silhouetted against the many fires still burning behind them.

---

"Did you hear that? It came from the passageway." Hillel stood facing the portal.

"What was it?" Malkiel asked.

"I do not know, but the sound is gone now." Hillel's concern was evident.

"Do you want to investigate?" Ozel asked.

"What? You mean, go in there?" Kalil could not believe his large friend would even consider this. The dragons' behavior had become so reclusive that he feared they would not want anyone buzzing around their hidden home, if indeed they had claimed it.

"Surely, why not?" Ozel shot back rather quickly.

Kalil simply motioned to Hillel, a gesture that seemed to indicate he would go along with whatever the latter decided.

Hillel looked away from the doorway, thinking to himself several long moments. Then, turning to his friends he said, "I am ready to go in if you all want to join me."

Kalil's head and shoulders drooped, clearly showing his level of frustration. Part of him wondered why he could not have found other friends who were less likely to head off into potentially dangerous situations.

The four were in agreement and cautiously began the journey through the portal. The colors at first caused them to feel dizzy as they swirled and gradually faded into the blackness of the center. They continued on and all unsheathed their swords. The blue flames gave these angels at least a little light as they flew. When the cave opened up in front of them, they navigated the Crypsis slowly, the blue flames from their swords dimly lighting the obstacles before them. They noted the dots of orange light beneath them, millions of fires with no explanation as to why they were there.

In the distance Malkiel saw it first, as he was flying at just the right height and in the right orientation to see a large orange glowing mass in the distance, beyond the maze of dark towering spires.

"Halloo, over here!"

Seeing the others heading his way, he flew toward the glow. He flew past many of the peaks until only a few remained between himself and the undulating glow before him. Then he heard the sound of Lucifer greeting his choir.

---

"Fellow seraphim!" The crowd grew quiet beneath the words of Lucifer their Commander. The only sounds were the popping and crackles of the various warming fires that dotted the ground among the assembly. "We are about to embark on a journey that will change the very nature of creation. This darkness that we have found, this Crypsis, has changed us, and it has shown us that what we were made to be can be changed. Just look at our skin and eyes! We have each grown our own scaly defenses, we need no one to defend us. We have become self-sufficient. The darkness has made us stronger, and this darkness will reach out and change the rest of creation. We will be the instruments of darkness!"

———————

The four fiery friends nestled together about half way up one of the steeples. Only Ozel looked around the edge to watch the commander as he spoke. "We must report this to Uriel," Ozel said as he pulled himself back behind the edge.

"I cannot believe what I am hearing. He is not thinking right," Malkiel observed.

"No, he is not. Let us go back and report what we just heard." Hillel motioned for them all to head back. "I think it is fair to say that we need to get out of here unnoticed."

Kalil sped past him on his way back to Paradise.

———————

Michael and Uriel split up and made their way to the other Archangels, spreading the news. Each commander sent scouts to round up all troops scattered in Heaven and on the Earth. They worked quickly; time was short.

———————

Heading back through the portal, the four could hear that strange sound again, a flowing, rushing sound, and it seemed to be growing louder. Exiting the opening, they flew to the opposite side of the canyon. Hillel landed and watched the opening, hearing the sound growing louder as time passed. The other three joined him, crouching behind an outcropping of rock,

"What is happening?" Ozel asked Hillel, not expecting an answer.

Just then, dragons began pouring from the opening in a steady stream of dark leathery wings flapping furiously. The Crypsis seemed to be coughing up all its inhabitants in one steady stream. The darkness of the flow of dragons scarcely allowed light to get through them. Not wanting to be noticed, the four angels remained still, watching the horde advance from their hole.

The thick line of dragons leaving the portal began branching out. As many of the now dark creatures traveled throughout Paradise, others shot through the portal to Earth on their respective missions. Shouting from the skies, "Lord Lucifer, the mighty one, demands a meeting in the throne room at midday! All hosts of heaven are commanded to attend!" This message was shouted throughout Paradise and Earth, wherever angels gathered.

---

It had taken some time to calm the hosts, as the message being called out by the Seraphim sounded strange indeed, but all of the choirs of Cherubim were ready on time and each grouping flew silently into the throne room, taking their places. They were all dressed in their full parade armor, swords and shields by their sides.

Inside the throne room, Michael gazed across the expanse as the angels flew in. He could not help noticing how united and orderly they had become, and much of this order came about under the leadership of the former Commander, their new enemy. Each grouping had taken on attributes of its leader in new and unexpected ways. Some angels of Uriel's group had begun their transition from their original orange flames toward the pure blue of their leader.

Remiel's group was absolutely silent, preserving their thunder for appropriate times. Michael had seen a display of what Remiel's thunder could do-so powerful was the thunder he produced, he could only imagine the things this choir had learned. They seemed so conscious of their sonic abilities that they maintained strict silence when not using it.

It was still well before the appointed time when all the choirs were fully assembled. Each archangel called his choir to attention, then placed them at ease to wait for midday. Michael broke from formation to survey the choirs, and taking to the air, headed for one of the large rear balconies near the main entrance.

---

Lucifer and the other Seraphim gathered outside the throne room. They were early, and Lucifer wanted to bring them in after the other angels had assembled. "Where are the other choirs?" Lucifer asked one of his advisors.

"I just received a report that they all gathered earlier and are already assembled in the throne room."

"How can that be? We did not give them that much notice."

"Maybe they knew before you sent the word out?" The advisor wondered out loud.

Lucifer was baffled at the promptness of the Cherubim, as he had expected some form of disorder since he had given them so little notice, and he wanted to confuse them by putting the leadership off balance so he would have a better chance of swaying them to his side. Now he would have to be more persuasive, he would really have to press his case. "Get this group ready to go!" Lucifer ordered, flatly staring at the temple. "...and get me a report from the throne room."

"Yes sir," the advisor said as he turned to a scout, and with a nod, the scout was on his way.

---

As Michael surveyed the waiting hosts of heaven, he saw something unexpected in the center section where the dragon choir would normally assemble. There now stood several hundred Seraphim, still as colorful as the day they were created. Apparently this group was not siding with Lucifer and his rebellion, and had not spent much, if any, time in the Crypsis.

Just then he noticed the dark-skinned Raguel flying toward the balcony where he stood. Raguel's flight conveyed the feeling of majesty and elegance unlike any of the other archangels. As Raguel set down on the balcony, he was the portrait of calm assurance. Surely this one had spent much time before the throne, his radiance was evident. Might and justice shone in his eyes.

"Quite an impressive display the choirs make," Michael said as Raguel approached.

"Yes, they have all done so well, we should be proud of them all."

"Indeed, what's on your mind?" Michael asked and waited, knowing Raguel always carefully selected his words.

"The Seraphim in attendance concern me. I believe Lucifer presents some sort of threat, and if I am right, I believe we need to remove these Seraphim from where his choir will be standing."

"Remove them? What do you have in mind?" Michael leaned on the balcony railing, placing his foot on the lower rail.

"I've talked with the other Archangels, and we believe we should split them up and move them into the other choirs," Raguel said.

Michael looked back toward him. "You want to hide them?"

Raguel paused, thinking over the possibilities, "That is correct. I would like to hide them."

Michael stared over the balcony again at the seraphim, noting that they seemed edgy.

"We do not know what is going to happen here, but if your hunch is right, and I think it is, we need to protect our Seraphim friends. I agree with the rest of the Archangels. How may I help?" Michael asked.

"I will see to it," Raguel said, backing away, lifting off the balcony with his massive ebony wings, then turned and swooped down to the floor of the throne room. Michael watched as the powerfully-built archangel dispersed the Seraphim, moving them into the other choirs, hiding them in the crowds of the Cherubim.

---

"They are assembled in the throne room and waiting," the Seraphim advisor noted, standing at attention. The messenger was walking back to his place in the formation.

"Very well, get this choir in there. We do not want to keep them waiting any longer," Lucifer said, exhaling a deep dark smoky breath, his large yellow eyes shifting to the direction of the temple.

## Chapter 26

# *Accusation*

The Seraphim choir was always impressive, and the formation flying of these massive creatures was awe-inspiring. With their changed countenances, their movements took on a strange foreboding appearance. They seemed dark, even here where there were no shadows. The familiar sound of Lucifer's wings beating the air in a slow pulsating drone resonated through the vast room, growing louder as he emerged through the doorway, very slowly, then hovered in place. He needed no balcony to survey his troops.

Michael noted the scales that now covered Lucifer's back and sides appeared to be a hard plating, similar yet much more robust than the scales he had seen on some of the fish the Creator had made. No, these scales had a thickness and sheen that made them seem almost metallic, completely hiding the jewels beneath, if indeed the jewels were still present. Lucifer's change was complete.

Michael continued to watch the Seraphim leader, looking for any indication that the previously-hidden dragons had caught Lucifer's gaze. If he had seen them, he did not let it show.

The Seraphim commander moved to the head of his choir as they settled into place. Michael flew down to reach the front of his choir joining Lucifer and the other archangels in their appropriate places. Metatron stepped forward to address the hosts.

"Hosts of heaven, thank you for your efforts to gather so quickly."

Lucifer wondered what else this gathering might be for, as he had called the meeting without informing Metatron. Surely there must have been another reason for the troops to gather, since they must have begun to gather before he had sent out his messengers.

"Lucifer would like to address the Creator and all of you." Metatron announced.

Lucifer was surprised and, after the briefest of pauses, made his way to the top of the stairs, purposefully diverting his eyes from the throne. Instead, as he ascended the stairs, he looked at the Seraphim he had placed as guards. They had grown larger and were completely engrossed in watching the manifestation of the Creator on the throne, so much so, that Lucifer could only groan under his breath as he shook his head slightly, regarding the four angels as being under some sort of spell and regretting his decision to place them there. They seemed to be completely unaware of the vast crowd that had gathered.

Reaching the top step, Lucifer moved to the middle, in front of the throne and turned to face the Creator. For the first time since he had begun his questioning of this Being's motives, he stood in the presence of his Creator. As he gazed past the sea, the lamp stands and the burning stones, and into the fires of the One in front of him, he began to experience a warmth flooding into his being. It felt good. He had missed the sensation of warmth. He glanced to one of the four Seraphim around the throne, wondering what he was murmuring. He felt himself being pulled into the light of Creation. He became aware that he could stop his rebellion now, for he knew the Creator was inviting him back. If he continued with what he had planned, there would be no turning back. It was as though the Creator himself held out his hand of acceptance.

Lucifer's heart began to soften. He slowly closed his eyes. His jaw clenched, and his countenance again took on a shrouded look. Regaining his composure, he said in a loud voice, "You have made all of the heavens, and You have made the Earth. You instructed us to worship only You, on the day You created us. Then You made Man. You made him in Your very image, a clay reproduction of Yourself, and now You-" Lucifer's body now bristled with fury, and raising one arm, he pointed a dark talon at the One on the throne, his eyes still closed, and shouted, "Now You want us to kneel before this idol and worship before it!"

A hush fell over the angelic hosts that filled the throne room, for they could not believe their former Commander was pointing his finger at the Creator!

Lucifer continued, "I will not do it! We are made of fire and water, and this man is made of clay! We are better than him." He turned to face the angelic hosts, opening his eyes wide. "And I believe none of these here want to worship this man either." Looking over to Michael, Lucifer extended his hand, inviting the angelic prince to join him.

Michael proceeded up the steps, slowly, his head down. The other Archangels exchanged glances, for they had not expected Michael to join Lucifer's cause, not *this* cause.

Michael reached Lucifer's side, lifted his head in the direction of the throne, and while facing his Creator, opened his eyes wide. His armor began to glow as if the very fire of Elohim emanated from it.

Lucifer, turning Michael away from the Creator, stooped down to peer into his eyes. "My brother, you were not created to worship that clay idol, you were created for far more. Can you not see it? You were made to rule millions, not grovel before clay." Lucifer's eyes were pleading.

Michael in turn searched Lucifer's eyes, looking for something. The two stared at each other for several seconds. Having not found what he searched for. He whispered, "Who is like Elohim? Are you like Elohim?"

Lucifer pulled his head back, trying to understand where this question came from. A look of horror covered his entire being. Gathering his thoughts again, he knew he had to counter this question in the strongest terms possible. Out of the bowels of Lucifer, the dragon leader, shot the words, "I am better than Elohim. My throne will be above that of the Creator's. While He plays with his clay dolls, I shall lift my throne far above His. None shall rule over me, none shall.....",

"Stop!" Metatron called out.

Lucifer thought Metatron had addressed him, only to now feel a blistering sting on the underside of his neck. It was then that he noticed Michael's flaming blade, cutting a gash into the tender skin. Never before had Lucifer seen such anger in the eyes of a Cherubim.

Michael pulled the sword back, the gash healed quickly in the presence of Elohim.

Lucifer's countenance grew so dark that he appeared to completely absorb light, and darkness was covering him. His eyes turned even more pale and jaundiced as the pupils narrowed to sinister slits, he continued looking intently at Michael. "I can see, my brother, that you have chosen sides."

"You are mistaken, it is you who have conjured up your own side, taking a stand against the very One who made you. No, I have not changed sides, I am exactly where I shall always be."

Turning to the left and to the right, Lucifer held out his hands motioning for the other Archangels to follow him. Each one shaking his head, they stood firm.

As he then turned to face the choirs, Lucifer rose to his hind feet, arms outstretched, wings completely unfurled.

"Hosts of heaven, this is your opportunity to follow me, I will not ask again." With that, Lucifer slowly lifted from the stage, the roar of his wings more menacing than before. Quickly gathering speed, he flew out of the throne room. The other Seraphim Generals rose from the floor and lead their troops out of the throne room in formation.

Once the Seraphim had left, Metatron addressed the throne room. "If any of you wish to follow Lucifer, you are dismissed at this time."

Reluctantly, a small number of Cherubim from each choir stepped from the ranks. Their compatriots begged them not to go. They felt compelled to follow the former Commander. One by one over five hundred flew out of the throne room, meeting up with Lucifer and the others outside.

Michael, returning his sword to its sheath, began walking back down the steps when Metatron called out, "Michael, please come back".

Michael stopped, turned, and rejoined Metatron.

"Michael, today everything has changed. Today the Kingdom of Elohim has suffered at the hands of one angel, today iniquity was found in Lucifer's heart. Today his identity has changed, he has become an enemy of Elohim. He turned his heart completely away from his Creator, hardening it. Today he has become Satan; he will no longer be called Lucifer, for he no longer bears light but only darkness.

'He will be your adversary, as he will strike at the very ones you have been charged to protect. You must defend the image of the Creator from this Satan."

Metatron paused to address the throng of angels, "Hosts of heaven, you are all that remains of the former host, fully one-third of your number has become your enemy." He then spoke the words they had heard once before.

"Do not allow your hearts to harden,
remain soft and pliable
before your Creator.

'Do not close your eyes,
always allow the light of heaven
to pass through them,
for only His light can illuminate
your inward parts.

'Do not stop listening
to the Word of the Creator
and His Spirit,
always allow Him to guide you
in all you do.

'These words were not heeded by those in whom iniquity was found. Fix your eyes on the task at hand: iniquity must be purged from Paradise." Metatron turned to Michael. "Please kneel before your Elohim."

Without hesitation Michael dropped to one knee, head bowed before his Creator. As Elohim began to speak, the entire assembly dropped to their knees. Thunder erupted from the throne, "Viceroy of heaven, today you are given a new title. Today you are Michael, Captain of the Armies of Paradise."

The hosts leapt to their feet and erupted in glorious cheers. Michael lifted his head to again face the throne. The warmth of the fires of Elohim filling his being, dancing on his skin.

Metatron moved to his side. "Arise," he said quietly, then looking to the troops, shouted, "Hosts of heaven, I present to you, Michael, Captain of the Armies of Paradise."

Michael arose, turned to face the assembly, wings completely outstretched. Pulling the burning sword from its sheath with his right hand, he lifted it into the air and shouted,

"WHO IS LIKE ELOHIM?"
"NO ONE!" Shouted the assembly as with one voice.
Again he shouted, "WHO IS LIKE ELOHIM?"
The troops shouted again, this time much louder. "NO ONE!"

233

"Praise be to the Creator of the Heavens and Earth! Lift your voices to the King of glory!" Michael directed the assembly.

The entire throne room began praising and worshiping the One seated on the throne as only angels could.

———————

Outside the throne room, the Cherubim defectors gathered with the Seraphim horde. From behind them emanated cheers and praise.

'I will get everyone back to our world,' Azazel told his commander.

"Very well," Lucifer responded coldly.

One of the dragons asked under his breath, "What happens next?"

Lucifer's pale yellow eyes were not diverted from the temple as he rubbed his freshly healed neck, and all he said was "War."

# Chapter 27

# *Preparation*

The morning was crisp, the fruit sweet and tart, the kind of tart that got him right under his ear, behind his jaw. "It's perfect," Adam exclaimed as he handed half of the peeled orange to his bride.

Removing a slice, she brought it to her mouth and bit. "Ooooooo," and a big smile lighted her already glowing face. The two walked hand in hand through the lush grass beneath the fast-growing orange grove. They had become accustomed to the animals gathering to see them.

"Good morning, Hyenas" the woman said. The two animals seemed almost to giggle at the greeting, as they both bowed their heads in respect.

———————

The angels never expected the field to be used for this purpose. It served quite well as a parade field, and now Satan and his choir had gathered at the far end. They were waiting for the choirs of Elohim to meet them in battle. Several hundred of the Seraphim army had brought huge kettle drums and were pounding out a deep rhythmic beat. Satan paced back and forth, slowly, patiently.

The Cherubim formations began flying into view. Each, again fully equipped.

---

Michael stood in the throne room waiting. Metatron approached him quickly, stopping as he passed by to say, "The Creator wants to speak with you alone. The favor of Elohim rests on you, Captain."

"Thank you, sir," Michael responded quietly.

He knelt before the throne, waiting for his Creator to speak. As Metatron neared the side doorway, he turned, looking at the lone Archangel kneeling before his Creator. Before leaving, Metatron felt a tear rolling down his cheek as he whispered, "He has risen to his proper position on his knees."

"Michael," Elohim thundered.

"Yes, my Lord."

"You have been chosen to lead My armies. Your assignment is to throw down Satan and all that stand with him. You are to throw them to the Earth, and seal the doorways leading to my Paradise, for a season."

"I understand," Michael responded, still kneeling.

"I will not allow the enemy's life to be extinguished, I *will* protect his life. Do you understand?"

"Yes, my Lord."

"There will be casualties on both sides, but injuries will heal quickly in my Paradise. However, this will not be the case in the other worlds."

Michael wondered what He could mean.

"Do you have any questions?"

Michael paused for a moment, emotions welling up inside him. He spoke quietly, in the softest of whispers, "I was not made for this. Lucifer," he paused, "now Satan, was made to be the captain of Your host. Who am I that I should lead Your army? I do not wish to fail You. My heart is faint with the knowledge of what lies ahead, to battle with the one whom I once called Commander, the one who is better than I am."

"Michael, you were made for everything I will ever ask you to do. Every decision and choice was taken into consideration before anything was created. You are in exactly the position which you were created for, nothing has escaped my planning because I have created everything perfectly."

"Did you know that Lucifer- sorry, I meant to say Satan- would choose to disobey you, to rebel?"

"I knew he could choose that, and I planned for it, just as I planned for your choice, whatever it may have been. I did not create him to be evil, but this was a path he chose. It would be impossible to provide freedom without allowing for evil. Without freedom there is no possibility for love. So, in order to have the possibility for love, there must also be the possibility for evil. Let me say it another way, love must be chosen, and therefore, there must be the ability to choose not to love, which is what Satan chose."

"I understand," Michael paused briefly then said, "There is one more matter. We outnumber Satan's troops, yet they are much more powerful than we are. Can we win?"

The swirling green cloud seemed to grow in intensity as the Creator spoke to the heart of this. "I will never give you an assignment you cannot accomplish. Gather your strength from me, release it at the right time. Michael, rally the troops to me, as you did when the accuser appeared, and they will fight in my power as well. Apart from Me, you can do nothing." The Creator paused, allowing this creature to absorb the meaning of His words. "Michael, arise. Captain, your army awaits."

Michael turned, heading for the exit. As he flew, the Spirit of Elohim spoke to his heart, "I have given Uriel a plan, ask him about it."

"Yes, sir," Michael responded.

---

He flew from the temple over the Cherubim standing in formation. More were approaching the field, and he noticed Uriel's choir encompassed the rear and sides of the entire group. "Now where is Uriel?" He directed his keen vision down, searching the grounds. "There he is," he said, and swooped to the field, landing several yards from his target.

Uriel saw Michael's final approach and motioned for one of his group commanders to place the choir in position. He walked toward Michael, quickly arriving at his Captain's side.

"Greetings Captain!" Uriel gave his friend a smart salute.

"Thank you, Uriel. Your preparations seem to be going well." Michael leaned toward him, "I hear you have a plan."

"I do sir, how did you know?"

Michael smiled knowingly, "What is it?"

Uriel, intrigued, continued, "I have stationed my choir to the rear of the other choirs. As the troops advance I would like to..." The two walked together as Uriel explained. Michael motioned for the other Archangels to join them. The group worked together, making sure each Archangel knew where to be and what to expect. War had never been experienced before, so experts did not exist.

Many minutes went by with the group going over various aspects of Michael's strategy and Uriel's plan. The two ideas seemed to fit together perfectly. They went over as many possible contingencies as they could think of, trying to ensure victory. Once they had finished, Michael addressed the group saying, "Friends, we fight not for ourselves nor for our glory. We fight for the Creator and His glory. Now let us purge this rebellion from Paradise by the power of Elohim."

"Amen," came the unanimous response from the Archangels.

"Let us get on with it, and please be sure each individual in each of your choirs keeps his heart focused on Elohim."

The group broke up, leaving Michael and Uriel to finalize their plans as the rest of the Archangels made their way to their respective choirs.

————

"Send a messenger inviting their leader to the center of the field for a discussion," Satan told an advisor. The messenger leapt to the air without hesitation. Heading straight to the Cherubim's front line, so intent on his mission, he had not seen the Cherubim's interceptor coming from the side. He was blindsided by Raguel, who tumbled the small dragon to the ground with a thud. Raguel landed within inches of his face, sword tip just piercing between the small dragon's newly-developed scales.

"What business have you on this side of the field?" Raguel asked.

"I have a message from Lucifer to whomever is leading your army." The panting and bewildered dragon answered.

Raguel grasped the serpent neck allowing the dragon to stand, sword still to his throat, "That would be Michael. What is the message? I will see that he receives it."

"Lucifer is requesting that Michael come to the center of the field for a discussion," replied the small dragon.

"To discuss what?" Raguel pressed slightly harder with the sword.

"He did not tell me! I gave you the message as he gave it to me!"

"Very well, I will relay your message, and his name is no longer Lucifer. It is now Satan, by order of Elohim. You can let him know that." Raguel turned to leave.

"You will be sure Michael gets the message?" The desperate dragon clawed at the ground to help himself up.

"I told you I would."

———————

"Raguel, what was that all about?" Michael asked, as he watched the little dragon hurry back to the opposite side of the field.

"Satan is requesting a mid-field discussion with you."

Michael and Uriel looked at each other, puzzled. "All right then," the former responded. "Would you two care to join me?"

"Yes sir," both said without a moment's hesitation.

———————

Satan approached the center of the field, looking across to the other side, "Are those dragons siding with our enemy?" He couldn't believe his eyes. A small group of several hundred Seraphim were finding a place in the center of the front lines.

"Oh my God! It is!" Semyaza responded, at first believing his eyes were lying to him.

"Please refrain from using *that* term..." Satan shook his head, "Perfect, now my Generals are calling Him God!"

----

The three neared the center of the field. Satan was already waiting, with two of his generals further back. Michael, a short distance from Satan, spoke to his companions, "You two wait here." Both fell behind, yet remained watchful, Raguel folding his arms in front of his chest, and the two watched their new captain walk to confront this shadow that had once been their leader.

"Ah Michael, so you are leading the Cherubim now. You were the right one for the position. As I said in the throne room, you were meant to lead millions."

"What did you want to talk to me about?" Michael asked, looking at his former leader, eyeing his new scales closer.

"Slow down, little Cherubim, unless you really *want* this war." Satan looked away, waiting for a response. Having received none, he continued. "Don't you see that you're made to lead, not made to serve?"

"I am made to serve my King, to carry out His will." Michael would have no patience if Satan only wanted to restate the same argument.

"Well, now Elohim has made man your King, you're serving Him now."

"I am serving Elohim, and Him alone."

"You're going to end up like those Seraphim in the throne room, they're bound to the throne, never to escape."

"They are there by choice."

"Is that what *He* told you?"

"It is the truth."

"Can't you see that His will is to bind you, lock you up, and throw away the key? He doesn't want you to become all you *can* be."

"Can you hear yourself? When did *you* become judge over the Creator. You think you know more than He does?"

"I became wiser, I question His motives, I question His so called 'plan.' If He had planned all this, we would have known about it. He is making it up as He goes, and I'm spoiling His plan."

"He has planned for every choice you could ever make. Every choice you could possibly make leads to His victory."

"We're not getting anywhere with this." Satan could not believe the level to which Michael trusted the Creator.

"You have no right questioning the very One that created you." Michael's eyes burned with indignation. "He knows your beginning, and He knows your end."

"Yeah? You think He knew this would happen? You think He knew my throne would replace His, that His creation would exceed

Him in greatness? Do you think He knew you would fight me and lose?"

"You cannot win."

"Arrogant little angel, aren't you?"

"I speak the truth. The entire creation does not have the power you think you have. Your pride in yourself has blinded you to the true greatness of the One you would seek to fight. You try to lower Him to the level of one that has a beginning. *He* has no beginning, *He* is uncreated. You cannot defeat Him without first being like Him, and you are not like *Him* at all. There is no way you can win. I have been instructed to defeat you, and throw all of you out of this place, and that is what I will do."

"Did He *really* say to throw us out?"

"Yes, he did."

Satan looked toward the Cherubim army. "You are willing to put all of them at risk, for Him? You know we're stronger than you."

"There is no risk, but if there were, I would be willing to risk everything for Him."

"Everything?" Satan asked with a sideways glance.

"Everything." Michael's resolve was unwavering.

"Then let's see where this goes. I'll see you on the field." Satan turned his scaly back and began to move toward his troops.

"Yes, you will." Michael called out.

"Oh," Satan did not bother to turn and look at Michael. "and tell my traitorous brothers, we're coming for them first."

Michael turned and leaped to the air, his two companions quickly joining him.

"Did he take the bait?" Uriel asked quietly.

Michael nodded.

## Chapter 28

# War

"He is unshakable," on one side Lucifer, now called Satan, growled, completely frustrated. "Send messengers to the Generals. Tell them we attack the enemy Seraphim first."

"Yes sir," the advisor left quickly.

---

On the other side, the Army of Light, as all the Archangels defending Elohim soon assembled: Archangels Michael, Gabriel, Uriel, Raguel, Remiel, Raphael, and Zerachiel.

"Let the other Archangels know the final details to the plan, and be sure they are ready," Uriel and Raguel said as they quickly moved through the choirs, finding the Archangels and filling them in on the last details.

The kettledrums still boomed in the background, the rhythmic beat escalating everyone's tensions. The Seraphim began hitting their hands against their chests, the new scales causing an irritating rattling sound, in rhythm with the background of drums. At random, individual Seraphim dragons breathed fire into the air.

―――――

The messenger, unsure of himself, approached Lucifer. Welcomed by his leader, he gained the nerve to deliver the news. "Sir, Elohim has changed your name."

Lucifer's face contorted, "What?"

"Elohim has declared you are no longer to be called Lucifer. Your new name is Satan."

"They're calling me enemy?" Satan looked across the field to his adversaries. "Good! I *AM* THEIR ENEMY! I *AM* Satan!" He began laughing, the uncomfortable advisor started to laugh. Then Satan's laughter began to change, taking on a disturbed, sinister, altogether evil nature. The advisor, thinking it best not to crowd his Commander, backed away several steps.

―――――

Uriel had split his troop into three parts: one third moving to the right and another third to the left, into the trees that surrounded the field on either side. The last third remained in place to the rear of the Cherubim. Keeping low to the ground, they used the other Cherubim as cover. They made sure to move slowly. The hosts of heaven all had incredible eyesight so care had to be taken to avoid detection, as any sighting by the adversary could reveal their plan.

―――――

The arrangement of the Cherubim choirs placed Michael's choir in the center, and to either side stood Raphael and Raguel's choirs. Directly in front of Michael's choir were the Seraphim(L) angels who remained on the side of light.

———————

Standing on the balcony of the throne room, Gabriel pulled forth an eight-foot long corkscrew-shaped silver shofar that was slung on his back. Overlooking the field, his eyes riveted to his Captain.

Michael and his choir began to walk toward the center of the field. Above them they could hear the war cry of the shofar, clear and strong, a long low bellow leading to an upturned pitch, then echoing across the field. Several miles separated the Army of Light from the Army of Shadow. Michael's choir split as it advanced around the waiting Seraphim(L) troops who held their position.

Satan, seeing his adversary advance, began walking as well. Both armies began slowly moving toward each other.

Once Michael's choir had advanced past the Seraphim(L) troops the flanking choirs of Raguel and Raphael moved toward the center completely surrounding the Seraphim(L). Once surrounded, the Seraphim(L) and Cherubim groups moved together as a unit, advancing behind Michael's troops toward the field's center.

———————

Satan spoke to one of his Generals, "He is trying to protect the traitors. Azazel, show them there is no protection for anyone that crosses us."

"Yes, Sir." Azazel rose into the air, summoning his choir to join him. The group's movement was that of a dark menacing swarm with Azazel in the lead. Heading across the field, the swarm looked like an undulating black cloud, pulsing with sinister intent. Reaching the Cherubim in short order, the swarm spread out over the opposing Seraphim(L) dragons, expecting to see a look of trepidation on their faces.

Instead, what they saw was the look of righteous indignation. Azazel spotted one of the Seraphim(L) looking directly at him, and it took a moment to realize this dragon was actually looking past him. Turning to see what was beyond, Azazel barely saw the blinding blue flash as it barreled into him, plummeting him to the ground. Wave after wave of flaming Cherubim streaked from the sides of the field. Azazel and hundreds of his troops tumbled in the midst of the Seraphim(L) dragons on the ground, waiting to have their way with the enemy. Azazel's attack was quickly routed, and the Seraphim(L) were joined by the surrounding Cherubim in carrying the wounded enemies to the portal, flinging them to the Earth.

Blue flames shot through the sky, millions of them, like arrows from the rear of the Cherubim masses. The fires of Elohim streaked toward the enemy, each with a will of it's own, veering left and right, each finding a target and plowing through it. Elohim's fires knocked Satan's bewildered dragons into the clutches of the waiting Cherubim and Seraphim who beat and slashed the dark dragons into submission, and while their actual wounds healed quickly, the exhaustion which the injuries brought on did not subside. The scaly Seraphim's strength was quickly sapped and each was thrown through the portal from Paradise to the Earth.

––––––––––

Adam and his Counterpart saw something, like lightning, hurdling toward Earth. Debris flying high into the air as the object struck the ground with such energy that small tremors rocked the ground. The object striking the ground pierced into the bowels of the Earth. Had they known it was alive, perhaps they would have marveled less. But this event was miraculous.

Another hit, then another, and another. These streaks of light, were so fast and powerful, as though they came from Heaven itself.

"What are they?" The bride asked, full of wonder.

Adam had no answer.

A steady line of Seraphim plummeted down from Paradise. The Cherubim had a hard time battling with a larger dragon and called out to Ozel, the one who had toppled Azazel, to come help. Landing just near the tail of the beast, Ozel grabbed it, lifting the dragon into the air, and began to fly in ever-tightening circles. Increasing the velocity with each revolution, he released the dragon, toppling it toward the Earth, another bolt of light in the night sky.

———————

From behind the Satanic forces, rows of undetected angelic warriors emerged from the thick woods, each carrying what looked like large oval shields, each warrior spaced a precise distance from the angel next to him. The shields, designed to radiate sound waves of specific frequencies, were each equipped with a pair of long spikes at the bottom, enabling the warrior to plant it in the ground. Each angel then could use one hand to hold the shield and the other to hit the shield's edge with the flat side of his sword, producing massive sound waves. The waves were so low in frequency that they could not be heard above the kettledrums that continued to drone on.

The sound's effect on Satan's Dragons, especially those toward the rear of the formation, was twofold. First, each began to feel nauseated as their internal organs vibrated with the waves of sound. Second, each had an inexplicable feeling of panic, causing them to want to run away from the wave, toward the center of the battle field. The forward troops kept advancing as the rearward troops continued to advance behind them. The effect was to move Satan's entire dragon horde forward and into the battle.

---

Satan, seeing his best warriors brought down by this surprise attack, sent his remaining dragons into the fray. His anger burned within him.

"There you are," Satan said to himself, watching Michael shouting orders to his troops. "I sent my best, headlong into battle, and you were waiting for them." Satan knew what he had to do.

---

Raphael saw Satan, the greatest dragon, hovering, studying the battle. He watched as Satan began to move, slowly at first, with some purpose. Then, building his speed, Raphael realized he was heading straight for Michael.

Gabriel zoomed past Raphael, heading directly for Satan. The thinly-built Gabriel intercepted the massive Satan.

"Stop right there," Gabriel shouted, shield in one hand, flaming sword in the other.

"Out of my way, little Archangel, I have an appointment with my destiny." Satan paused, "Hey, I thought you were the *messenger* of the Creator, what are you doing out here in this fight?"

"Delivering a message!" Gabriel flew headlong toward Satan, who spun around swatting the Archangel with his tail, catching him in the ribs. Loud crackling sounds emerged from Gabriel's body as he was tossed through the air. He quickly scooped the air with his wings, then used his momentum to bank back, around, flinging aside his ruined breastplate. Holding his side, he could feel the ribs moving back into position and mending quickly. He was undeterred. Shooting off in the pursuit of Satan, Gabriel recovered his shield and used it to block another tail swat while slicing a massive gash between his enemy's scales.

Satan turned, "Pesky little thing, aren't you."

"You have no idea," Gabriel replied.

Just then Satan saw a blue streak heading directly toward him, and as it approached he could tell it was Uriel rocketing through the air, coming to the aide of his fellow Archangel.

Satan braced for impact, but at the last instant the blue streak passed beneath him. He instantly became aware of the angel who had approached from another direction, but it was too late. Raguel's sword sliced into his midsection, sending him plummeting to the ground, fiery liquid oozing from the gash. Satan righted himself, looked back toward his troops. They were moving forward, and he did not know why. He new something must be driving them forward into the trap set by the Cherubim. He felt his belly healing, looked again at his troops, whose numbers were dwindling rapidly, and again rose to the sky.

Out of breath, Satan ordered his troops, "To the caves! My Seraphim dragons! To the caves!"

Liquid fire dripped from the healing wound, held shut with his left hand.

Michael's Cherubim army was unrelenting. They had orders from their Captain, and those orders would be fulfilled. As the Seraphim flew, retreating to their hide-out Michael's Cherubim continued to squelch any stragglers, taking them back to the portal and sending them crashing to the Earth.

The cave seemed to devour the swarm, as though sucking the dark mass into its black mouth. Into the cave they went, crashing into each other, blindly flying into the darkness, the Cherubim hot on their tails.

---

Michael's Cherubim warriors had not seen darkness before, certainly not like this. The Cherubim coming to the end of the tunnel slowed, wary of this place. They proceeded slowly, only the faint blue light from their swords providing any light. They listened, straining to hear the slightest sound from their quarry. In the distance a short blast of flames shot in the air. The Cherubim began making their way toward it, many hitting the tall spires hidden in the darkness. Once they had reached the place from which the blast had erupted, again they heard, farther off, another short blast and the rustling of membranous wings. Again the Cherubim moved toward the disturbance.

"Where are they?" One Cherubim asked in a quiet nervous tone.

"I do not know..." Peering into the inky blackness Jeremiel could barely make out two pail yellow eyes. As he lunged toward the dragon staring back at him in the darkness, bursts of flame began erupting all around them. He swung his sword wildly, and it found its mark. The blade exploded with a thunderous shock wave, the serpent's throat slashed, and the dragon who had been straining to see the Cherubim found himself propelled backward by the crash of sound driving him into several other dragons waiting to get in the fight. He grasped his throat: liquid fire leaking out between his fingers, while his wings worked hard to right him.

The bursts were brief, seemingly random, and with each blast Cherubim screamed in pain, the dragons' tail spikes and claws making short work of the angels. The Cherubim were thrown into a panic. What was happening? The random bursts of light played havoc with their ability to perceive reality. The torment was unrelenting.

An explosion of light filled the passageway, giving much needed help to those in the ambush. Hillel along with several hundred fiery angels, shot from the tunnel, clearly seeing the chaos ahead. He motioned orders to his fellow troops who began swirling in, around, and through the confusion, lighting the place up in an intense dance of orange and blue light, seizing the opportunity to silence dragons with their flaming swords as they shot through the air.

Jeremiel shouted to his fellow sound warriors, "Thunder you angels of light!" With that, massive peels of thunder were heard along with blasts and incredible booms.

It was the turn of Satan's dragons to be confused now. The great exploding sounds shook the very ground of the Crypsis, even the spires shook to their foundations. Other angels slashed at the dragons, opening wounds that refused to heal in this darkness.

Satan's numbers again began to dwindle, and in the light, the Cherubim could now see well enough to turn the tide. Each dragon was fighting with several Cherubim attackers. Between the light and the sound, his troops didn't stand a chance. Satan knew he had to get his troops back into the light, as their wounds were not healing here.

Grabbing a dragon by the tail with each of his hands and feet, Satan flew back through the tunnel, back into the light, realizing his dragon-angels could not fight with these horrific injuries. Once outside the tunnel, Satan placed his four companions on a hill where they could heal. His troops came swarming out of the Crypsis behind him.

Looking up, he saw Michael on a cliff overlooking the battle that continued in the light. Satan knew it was now or never. He began running, clawing the ground, trying to keep low, out of the sight of the other Archangels. Then at the last moment, he lunged and flew into the air.

On top of the mountain the brightness shone from Michael. Just then the Archangel heard the sound of something immense moving toward him, and turned quickly, bringing his shield around, knocking Satan's serpentine head away. Suddenly he felt the tail folding him in half, sending him careening into a large boulder. His breastplate tore open in several places as well as his flesh beneath it. The wounds were deep, and the pain almost unbearable. Liquid fire was spurting through the holes in his breastplate, running down beneath it.

---

Both armies, the Cherubim and Seraphim alike took notice of the battle raging on the mountain top. One by one they stopped and stared, some pointing out the fight for others to see. The battle had the appearance of darkness fighting the light.

Satan had landed twenty yards or so from Michael and began to laugh. "I can't win... That's what you said, wasn't it?"

Kneeling on the ground, holding his chest, Michael remembered the words Elohim had spoken in the throne room.

"Who is like Elohim?" The Archangel whispered to himself.

"What?"

Looking past Satan to his troops who now stood and watched, Michael spoke the words again, "Who is like Elohim?" This time he spoke louder, still to himself, the gashes and ribs healing beneath his hand.

Satan became indignant, "What is your obsession with that question?"

"It is the meaning of my name, and it is my battle cry." Michael got to his feet, the fire in his eyes grew more intense, and looking directly into the eyes of his adversary he shouted, "WHO IS LIKE ELOHIM?"

Michael paused to look out toward his troops once again. The entire battle had paused in this split second that seemed to last several minutes. Again he called out, louder than ever, "WHO IS LIKE ELOHIM!?"

'NO ONE!" Came the resounding reply, echoing through the cliffs.

"No one is like Elohim, no one will remove Him from His throne, no one will defeat Him." Michael's bronze skin began to shine. His tawny hair began to shimmer like pure gold. The fire of his sword turned to a light and yet brilliant shade of blue, matching the blazing inferno in his eyes.

Satan's eye's burned like sulphur, smoke billowed from his mouth and nostrils at every breath, as he stood fully erect, wings outstretched. Looking down at the Archangel, he again began to laugh. "You are pathetic, your devotion to your Creator disgusts me. I have no use for one such as you." He lowered himself, walking slowly toward Michael, who stood his ground. Satan, crouched within striking distance, his neck coiled back on itself like a great snake and said, "You were my brother, but no more." He lunged again at the Archangel, teeth bared, flames shooting from the dragon's nose and mouth.

Michael's shield met Satan's chin once again, bashing his face up and away, then with a yell and in a blindingly fast movement, he pushed the shield forward driving Satan's serpentine head up and away, exposing the tender, lower portion of the neck. This one powerful movement ended with Michael's sword pushing through Satan's neck.

Leaving the sword in place, Satan's throat impaled, Michael caught the dragon's tail as it again weakly tried to bash him into the rocks. Lifting the huge dragon, his powerful feathery wings strained under the load, and he carried Satan to the edge of Heaven. Pulling his sword from Satan's neck, Michael again lifted his enemy into the air, this time much higher and began spinning the serpent around himself. The two fighters were a blurred vortex in the sky, and the sound became so intense, like storm winds through thousands of trees, all other sounds were drowned out. When the release came, Satan tumbled to the Earth.

———————

"Oh, did you see that one?" Adam asked his bride.

"How could I miss it?" she answered. "This is incredible."

"Thousands of streaks of light cascading down all around us, shaking the Earth!" Marveling, Adam sat on the grassy hill, his little rabbit friend in his lap again, Woman holding the second rabbit.

---

In Paradise, once Satan had been thrown down, the final cleanup did not take long. Some of Satan's forces tried to escape, only to be caught by the swift Cherubim. Uriel called to Kalil, Hillel, Malkiel and Ozel to help seal the cave leading to the Crypsis. The righteous Seraphim angels, those on the side of light, piled boulders in the entrance, then helped with the fire to fuse the opening closed. They knew there were dragons still in the Crypsis, and the dragons that had been flung to earth would eventually get back there, but this would ensure they could not get back through this passageway. The newly-formed rock face glowed red hot as the group left.

# Chapter 29

# *Aftermath*

Metatron sat at his stone desk silently writing, a thick scroll almost finished. Not looking up, he held up one finger to Michael, who had just walked through the entrance to his office, and motioned for him to wait briefly. Finishing his writing, he placed his feather pen into its crystal inkwell, blowing on the ink to dry it, and rolling up the scroll. Then, dripping wax on the overlapping edge from one of the many candles burning in the room, he pressed his signet ring into the wax. Walking to a casement, he set the scroll in its place and said, "I see you have fulfilled your orders. Good work."

"Thank you, Sir."

"Those wounds must have been very painful."

"They have healed well, I only need to get this armor repaired." Michael exhaled deeply, walking the few steps to the window, peering out over the field that was once the parade field and had become a field of battle.

"No need to repair it, your new armor is next to you in the corner."

Turning to look, Michael saw the new armor, the metal pieces plated with yellow gold. The set was complete with a new sword, the hilt golden and the blade hot with blue flame.

Metatron had seen this before. Elohim had shown him this very scene, and here was the weary warrior standing before him.

"They are beautiful, thank you..." Michael said, his voice trailing off, and a sad expression on his face.

"What is wrong?" Metatron asked the question that had puzzled him since he had first seen the vision.

"We achieved victory for the kingdom; however, the cost was very high. I know we were in the right, but we have all lost friends today. This loss cannot be undone. Life cannot go back to the way it was."

The scribe nodded, sad too, for he also had greatly valued the former Lucifer and the other Seraphim angels. Metatron stepped away from the almost empty casement and looked toward Michael. After a brief pause, he changed the subject. "I have finished writing it all down," the scribe said with a smile, motioning to the scroll he had just put away.

Michael smiled, "Then it truly is finished."

"What will you do now, Michael?"

"I will return to the throne room, before heading back to Earth."

"Good idea."

Michael lifted the bundle from the corner and, cloaked in sadness, dismissed himself.

Metatron watched the archangel, the captain of the host of Paradise, leave. A voice whispered into his ear, "You have seen a true warrior. I am strengthening him even as he walks to Me."

---

Adam and his Counterpart made their way down the grassy hill, all the while staring in the direction of the dusty upheaval. Reaching the place where one of the streaks of light had struck the ground, they saw smoke that continued to rise from the broken Earth. Across the plain many of these craters were visible. Adam walked over to the hole and squatted down to move a few of the smaller chunks of Earth, when the ground began to shake. He quickly rose and took a few steps back. Both he and Woman looked all around at the quaking Earth and then at each other in confusion.

Then, hearing a new sound, they looked back to the hole to see a clawed hand emerging from the Earth. It grabbed the surface, struggling to pull itself up. Seeing this creature struggling, Adam quickly made his way over to help what turned out to be a huge dark dragon from the hole.

Looking stunned and off balance, the massive creature held his face in what were indeed claws, then arched his back, and six leathery wings unfurled. Two of the wings on one side appeared to be broken, a nasty cut oozed on the dragon's throat, and the scaled body showed many and various smaller cuts and punctures. Molten fluid flowed freely from the wounds.

"Are you all right?" Adam asked, "Here, let me help steady you."

The dragon spoke with a deep, raspy, gravel like tone, "Yeah, I'll be all right, give me a moment." The dark dragon struggled to maintain his balance. He grasped his throat, to ascertain that the wound was indeed healing very slowly in this place. "Who are you?" He asked, his eyes still covered.

"I am Adam, and this is my counterpart, Woman."

Satan froze. Slowly he slid his hand from his face, revealing his yellow eyes, and stood face to face with the objects of his hatred.

"Do you know who I am?" The scaled dragon asked.

"I do not know who you are, but I do know your kind." Adam answered in a very pleasant tone.

"...and what *kind* would that be?"

"You are one of the Seraphim dragons. Elohim told me he named your kind."

Satan's head nodded slightly, "That's right, what else do you know?" He could feel liquid fire leaking out between his fingers, at the spot where Michael's sword had cut through his voice box, injuring his once elegant voice.

"Nothing really. I have not often seen your kind." Adam's attention was diverted to the dragon's neck. "We can talk later, let me help you. You look as if you are having a hard time standing."

---

Michael arrived just in time to see the exchange between Adam and Satan. His troops were looking to him to see if they should intervene. Motioning for them to refrain, he watched the interaction as Adam and Woman walked away with the dark dragon. Michael followed at a distance, quietly calling several angels to accompany him. The remaining Cherubim stood watch, scanning the many craters for any signs of stirring. Slowly, one by one, injured dragons emerged, nursing wounds that would heal very slowly here on Earth.

It appeared to Michael that it would be several months before they could muster any kind of threat.

## Chapter 30

# Conclusion

"What? It can't end like this!" Jessica scanned the writing again, then scanned it for a third time. "This can't be right!"

Her eyes moved from the scroll as she felt the warmth of her angelic mentor entering the study.

"What's wrong with it, Jessica?" Michael asked.

Turning to face him, her face glowing in the light of his countenance, she leaned against the desk, "It's ending with Adam and Satan walking away together? Why would it end that way?"

"This is not the end. Do not forget that."

Michael reached for the scroll as his bright countenance faded. Quickly rolling the scroll back up, he gently slid it into its leathery case, then popped the lid back onto the end of the tube. "If you will excuse me, I need to get this back."

Jessica was confused, "What do you mean get that back? Aren't you going to leave it with me?"

"No."

"Why not? I need that!"

"No, you have finished with it."

"I need it to show people the original."

"Why? You interpreted it. You have the story right there on your computer."

"Right, but I need to be able to point to the original to show people where it came from, to show them I'm not crazy."

"That is not your concern."

"Yes, it is!"

"No, it truly is not. There are those that will read what you have written-translated- and believe. There are also those who will read what you have written and not believe, regardless of any proof you might have. They will not allow themselves to believe. What matters is that you completed this portion of your assignment. Now you need to move forward and distribute your interpretation."

"So I've interpreted a scroll, but I won't be able to show anyone the scroll itself?"

"That is right."

She had a thoughtful look on her face as she stared at the floor, "Proof doesn't matter."

"Right again. You will have to get used to the idea that Man's fallen opinions make no difference. There is only One whose opinion matters. If you please Him, whose opinion means more than His?"

Jessica looked back to the archangel, "But this project was all about getting this scroll out there, so the world would have it. I thought I would at least be able to have the scroll, you know, for the skeptics."

"The skeptics will never believe. They have picked up the playbook of the original skeptic, the original doubter. His philosophy leads them into the pride of their own minds. They hold themselves and their opinions and their logic up against belief in the all-knowing, all-powerful Elohim. They have lost, or, so we can hope, have merely laid down their sense of mystery, their ability to believe even when they cannot touch or see something."

Michael slid the scroll's case into his shoulder bag. As he tied it shut, he looked at Jessica, "Here is something to think about: only Satan, his forces, and Man, altogether, doubt the word of God. So on whose side is Man?"

Michael shook his head while he slung the bag over his shoulder. "You have much to do. You have much work ahead of you to get this story ready. I will not take up more of your time. Once you have finished, I will return." Michael bowed in his usual way as he began to fade from view.

Jessica shook her head slowly as she watched him blending with the surroundings. The moment when she could barely see him, she remembered something she had forgotten to mention. "Wait, I'm not sure how to distribute the book!"

A voice from where the Archangel once stood, or still stood, answered, "Isabella will help you. This is one of the reasons she is with you."

Just then the phone rang. Jessica walked toward the sound and lifted the receiver, "Hello?"

"Jessica, it's Sara."

"Oh," Jessica's mind paused to refocus on the phone call. "Sara? Barry's Sara? What's wrong? You sound like something's happened."

"Yes... something *has* happened."

"Are you alright? Is Barry alright?"

"Yes, we're fine. Actually, it's just that I had a dream two nights ago."

"Really? A dream? I don't understand."

"I would never have called you with this, but Barry thought I should. Just in case."

"Umm, ok."

"I'm sorry to startle you, but whenever I have this kind of dream something bad is coming."

"I still don't know what you're talking about Sara. Please, can you just tell me from the beginning?"

"Sure, I'll try. It was one of those dreams that was so real, but now I'm only remembering parts of it. Anyway, it started with you and the scroll you've been working on. I think you ate the scroll and spit it out or maybe vomited it onto a platter. I remember it looked like it was really hard to get it out, but you did it. Then, you began passing it out to a bunch of people.

"That sounds right doesn't it? Your work with the scroll was to distribute it to many people, right?"

"Yeah, that's right, that visual is kind of disgusting, but go on."

"Then I remember a pair of really big yellow eyes, only they were pale, like barely yellow. You know, almost like a sickly pale yellow?"

"Yeah, I get it, pale yellow eyes. Go on."

"In the dream, right after I saw the eyes, I heard a voice say, 'Leviathon is coming.'"

"Leviathon? You mean like a sea monster?"

"Yeah, in the Bible, in the book of Job, Leviathon is more like a sea dragon, but yes."

"You're saying a sea dragon is coming to Colorado? And what does that have to do with the scroll?"

"I'm not sure. I'm not even sure if the two are related, except that they were both in the same dream. Like I said, I wouldn't have called, but Barry thought I should."

"Sara, I'm glad you called, I'll do some research on this Leviathon thing and try to figure out what to do."

"I'll do the same from this end, and Jessica?"

"Yes?"

"Please take care, ok? And keep us posted?"

"I will. Thanks again for letting me know. Please let me know what you find out too."

"Ok, I will. Bye for now."

"Bye Sara."

48720834R00160

Made in the USA
Middletown, DE
29 September 2017